PERSONAL REASONS

PERSONAL REASONS

A NOVEL

DAVID ROY

authorHOUSE®

AuthorHouse™
1663 Liberty Drive
Bloomington, IN 47403
www.authorhouse.com
Phone: 1-800-839-8640

Published by AuthorHouse 12/16/2014

ISBN: 978-1-4969-5902-7 (sc)
ISBN: 978-1-4969-5903-4 (e)

Library of Congress Control Number: 2014922234

Chapter One

Faye Evans thinks I'm half deaf.

She stares at my face and shouts, "I can't tell you how much I appreciate you coming over and taking a look at this." She pauses and lowers her voice a little. "You're a dear man for doing so and I hope I'm not bothering you, but you need to get out more often anyway, Matt. It's not good for you to be alone so much."

I shrug and say nothing.

She asks, "Well what do you think? Is the plumbing bad?"

We are standing in her guest bathroom. It is small and pretty and it smells nice. The walls are covered with flowered paper, and ceramic puppies are lined up on little shelves above the stool. There is a green and yellow bird in a cage that hangs from the ceiling, and there is a weed growing out of the sink.

We are studying the weed.

I want to tell Mrs. Evans that she doesn't have to talk so loud, but then she will know that I have been ignoring her when she calls to me over the back yard fence. She is not a bad person. I don't want to hurt her feelings. I just want her to leave me alone.

"I don't think the plumbing is bad," I say as I walk to the sink and pluck the weed. I turn on the water and let it run for a moment to make sure the drain isn't clogged.

It isn't.

I turn off the water and toss the weed into a small ceramic trash can that looks clean enough to eat from.

"That's it?" she scoffs with a blush.

I nod.

"How did that thing get in there?"

I look at the bird, and he chirps at me.

"Do you clean his water dish in the sink?"

She nods.

"A seed probably got hung up in the p-trap and sprouted."

"Really!"

"Yup," I say as I turn and head for the front door. Mrs. Evans follows me down the little hallway and through her living room, which is also pretty and smells nice. I put my hand on the door knob and twist it.

"How about lunch? A cup of coffee?" she asks.

"Another time, maybe."

"Well, thank you so much. I'd like to repay you? There must be something I can do." She blushes slightly.

I turn and gaze at her. She is standing close to me. I smell her perfume and her body lotion. Her face is small and attractive. Her eyes are hazel and her hair is black. I've seen her in shorts out working her garden. I know gravity hasn't been too rough on her yet. I also know she would like to see more of me, but I don't think that's a good idea.

I want to be alone. I like it quiet.

She wants company. She likes to talk.

It wouldn't work.

"Come back for dinner tonight," she says. "I'll make whatever you like."

I smile. "There's something I gotta do tonight, Mrs. Evans."

I step out onto the front porch.

"Will you please call me Faye," she shouts.

I pause and glance at her.

"See you later, Faye." I smile, and then I turn and go down the steps on her porch. I angle across her front yard and slip through the rose bushes into my side yard.

It is eleven-thirty in the morning. The air feels damp and it smells of the river and houses and lawns, and of Mrs. Evans's rose bushes. I climb up the steps on my front porch and enter my house.

I'm alone and it's quiet.

I like it that way.

Faye Evans has had a crush on me for several years. She used to flirt with me even when my wife, Pam, was still alive. Pam thought it was funny. I thought it was crazy.

When Pam became sick, Faye Evans stopped flirting with me and did what she could to help out. And after Pam died, Faye waited six months before she stated hitting on me again. As I said before, she is not a bad person, she's just lonely and she talks too much. She has outlived three husbands. Each of them left her a small fortune. Her fixed income is way higher than mine.

I don't know what she sees in me, and I don't know what her intentions are beyond the bedroom. Could be she doesn't have any, but I get the feeling she does.

I also get the feeling she thinks I'm some kind of hero after what happened last week.

Believe me, I'm no hero, and what happened in the little corner store a couple blocks from here didn't change anything. The media made way too big a deal out of it. Maybe it was a slow news week, I don't know, but the story didn't deserve headlines and two minutes of television.

Especially when part of it wasn't true.

Thank God a cop in Tacoma shot himself in the foot while trying to arrest a suspected drug dealer. The media dropped my story like a dirty pair of shorts, and that was fine by me.

Now, I just need to do something about Faye. She wasn't always so bold. She used to drop hints and toss me suggestive looks. That's as far as it went. I never felt targeted, maybe curious, but I never felt I was centered in her gun sights, until recently, and I'm not sure what to do about it.

Maybe I should go visit my little brother down in Portland Oregon for a week or so. Let things cool off.

Or maybe I should take Faye up on the cup of coffee and tell her the truth about what happened in the corner store. That's what I'd prefer to do, but I have a problem with the truth.

I'm embarrassed of it.

Chapter Two

My wife, Pam, has been gone a year now, and my loneliness has become my comfort zone.

I don't see anything wrong with that. I'm not happy, but I'm getting by.

I spend most of my days tinkering with my 1973 Mach One Mustang. I keep it in the detached garage out back by the alley. It is silver with a blue stripe. The paint is a little rough, but the body is straight and most everything in the car still works, including the radio which I have tuned to a classic rock station out of Seattle.

I like the music of the seventies. I miss that era, especially the early part of it, and particularly 1973.

That was the year after I came home from Vietnam and met Pam. I think about her as I tinker with the Mustang. I hear the songs we fell in love to, and I relive some of the moments we spent together when we were young, and life was simple.

Pam was originally from Shreveport Louisiana. Her southern accent could defrost a refrigerator from a block away. In '72 she ran away from home with a Volkswagen bus load of hippies who were on their way to Southern California, but somehow they wound up in the Seattle/ Tacoma area where they ran out of money and their bus broke down. The group split up. It was pretty much a fend-for-yourself situation. Pam was beautiful and smart. She was a survivor. When I met her in late '73, she was waiting tables in a hippy restaurant that I used to sober up in.

Funny how many times I'd sobered up in that restaurant without noticing her until the day she was the one who served me a cup of coffee.

Funny how I never met any of her family, but she talked about them all the time. Her father was in the oil industry. Her mother was a school teacher. Her two sisters were at LSU. Pam didn't invite any of them to our small marriage ceremony, and she never notified them of her illness either.

Sometimes while I'm working on the Mustang and thinking about Pam, I wonder if I shouldn't try to contact her family. Now-a-days it wouldn't be that hard a thing to do, but I've not got around to it yet because I'm not sure if Pam would want me to.

She talked about them, but she never acted as though she missed them or ever wanted to see them again. That part of Pam's life is mysterious, and knowing Pam, she kept it secret from me for one of two reasons.

Either it was painful to her, or she didn't feel it was significant to our relationship.

Whatever her reason, I'm okay with it.

I just seem to think about it more now than I did when she was with me.

I wonder why.

Some days I spend more time in the garage than I feel I should. Maybe I'm hiding from the world, but I don't think so. I think It's more a matter of feeling close to Pam, and that's where I want to be. I relive special moments with her. We had a good life together, and I get all caught up in it until something brings me back.

Today it's a train rushing by on the tracks out back on the other side of the alley. The ground trembles slightly, and the air fills with noise.

I glance out the window and see the light fading in a pale fall sky. I put my tools away and lock up the garage.

It is six when I enter my house.

I'm not sure what all I did after I fixed Faye's plumbing this morning.

I know I did more than tinker with the Mustang. I think I started a load of laundry, checked the mail, and took the garbage out. I hope I moved the laundry from the washer to the drier. I do things without much thought to them anymore. Very few are important, so why should I waste brain energy on them, and lately, I don't have much of an appetite either. When I do feel hungry, I eat sandwiches and junk food. Stuff that I can microwave. I never learned how to cook because I never thought I'd have to.

I check to make sure my laundry is in the drier, and then I take a beer from the fridge into the living room and plop down in my leather recliner. I use a remote to turn on the TV.

I watch the news out of habit.

I really don't care what's going on in the world, or my country anymore. Far as I'm concerned, America is the greatest place to live in the whole world, but she is dying from an incurable disease. I can't help, so I don't worry.

I glance around my living room and realize that I have left everything the way it was when Pam was with me. Everything from the pictures on the wall to the chair I'm sitting in. Her clothes still hang in the closet, her purse on the door knob. Her underwear are still folded neat in her drawer. Her jewelry box sits on her nightstand. I've not moved one item from where she left it.

I miss her. We were together forty years. She was a hippy and I was an angry Vet.

It shouldn't have worked.

It did because we loved each other, and we never allowed anything to get in the way of our feelings. We wanted children but she was unable to have them. We thought about adopting, but never got around to it.

Pam was loving and caring.

I was calloused and mean.

She told me she was attracted to my mean spirit.

I told her I was attracted to her body.

The way I love to picture Pam the most, is the way I saw her that very first time-- carrying a cup of coffee, walking toward me in a soft cotton dress with a stream of morning light catching her just right and tracing the lines of her slender body. I remember the smell of her hair, and the tender look in her big blue eyes.

I find myself crying silent tears while I watch the world go haywire on TV. Wars and rumors of wars. Protests and unrest. Random shootings. The polar cap is melting, and the UN wants to take away our guns.

I use my remote to turn it off.

I know there is something I have to do tonight.

Something I'm not proud of, but I have to do it anyway.

I rub away my tears as I rise from the chair and walk upstairs to take a shower. I shave and dress in clean blue jeans and a button down shirt. My shoes are scuffed and worn. I need new ones, and I'm not sure where to buy them. A shoe store, I guess, but Pam had always bought my shoes. She knew what I liked to wear, and she always took care of it. I never gave much thought to where they came from. I just wore them. That may sound funny or stupid, and maybe it is, but I know it was one of those things she did for me out of love, and it saddens me to think about it.

I feel odd at times. I'm sixty-two and I have to learn how to take care of myself all over again. I worked on bridges in Tacoma, and I worked on drilling rigs in Alaska. I worked hard all my life, and I retired as a Rig Manager. We bought this old house and fixed it up. We own it free and clear. Pam was good at saving and investing money. I have enough money to live fairly comfortable for another twenty years or so, as long as I'm careful.

I retired at sixty. Pam and I were supposed to finish growing old together....

That's all I'm going to say about that right now.

I lock up my house and fire up my Chevy truck. I take River Road into Tacoma where I catch the I-five and head south to the mall. While I drive, I wonder if I should ask Faye to help me find a new pair of shoes. She would probably like that. It would be a date.

I could tell her the truth about what happened. Slip it in somehow during our conversation, just sort of toss it out there and see how she reacts.

She'll probably leave me alone after she hears the truth.

Maybe that's not a bad idea.

Chapter Three

The woman is thirty-four years old.

That is young enough to be my daughter.

Her name is Becky. Her eyes are dark green, and her hair is brown with streaks of ash blond running through it. She is pretty, a little over weight, and considered tall for her gender.

We meet up at the fountain in the Tacoma Mall. We act as though we don't know each other. We walk five feet apart, and don't make direct eye contact.

Becky is wearing blue jeans that fit her tight, and a yellow cotton sweater. She is chewing gum, and giggling.

The crowd is light on Wednesday night. We don't spend a lot of time around the fountain. I head off down the corridor that leads to the Sears store, and Becky follows me a few moments later.

I walk as though I'm going to Sears for a battery or something.

Becky window shops. She is still giggling.

At the Sears entrance, I turn left and exit the mall. I walk back to my truck and climb in. I fire it up.

Two minutes later, Becky climbs in and chuckles.

I idle out of my parking space and angle across the lot toward an exit.

"What's so funny?" I ask.

"Why do we have to meet like this?"

"Because it's not right."

She shrugs. "Who's to know we are lovers."

"We are not lovers," I growl.

"Then why?"

I think about it, and change the subject. "What's Eric up to? Has he tried to hit you?"

Becky says, "No. He'd like to, but he's going to beat you up first."

I already know this, and I'm not worried about it.

I tell her what I've been telling her for the last week. "You need to get away from him for good."

She shakes her head. "He won't touch me because of you."

"Don't be so sure of that," I say.

She smiles.

"It can't go on like this, Becky. It has to stop. You need to leave him and find someone who is nice and close to your own age to take care of you. Believe me, there are lots of young men who would love you if they knew you."

She thinks about that for a moment, and then she says, "You are my hero."

I pull my truck out onto Fifty-Sixth Street and go south. "Don't say that. You know what I mean."

She scoots closer to me, and presses her thigh against mine.

She puts a hand on my leg.

I lift it and move it away.

She folds her hands in her lap and looks out the window.

"Where we going?" she asks.

"Right back to your car if you don't behave yourself."

"I wanna talk."

"Go ahead."

"Not while we're driving."

"Want to eat?"

"Yes."

"Where?"

"Johnny's."

"Okay."

She smiles.

"I'm way too old for this, Becky."

She lifts her hand and runs her fingers through my hair.
I scowl.

"I love your grey hair. It's beautiful."

"It's a mess," I rasp. "Way too old for you."

"Lots of young women are attracted to older men."

I think about that and I have no idea if it's true or not,
so I decide not to say anything.

I drive to Johnny's out in Federal way. It's a family
seafood restaurant. The meals cost about the same as they
do in most fast food places. The beer, wine and mixed
drinks are standard. Nothing exotic. Several large aquariums
loaded with colorful fish are placed throughout the dining
room. They draw children like a magnet draws metal. The
crowd is thin on week nights, I figure we'll be safe here, no
one will know us.

It starts to rain as we go inside.

Just a soft, Washington State, September drizzle.

We get a booth in back by the windows. Becky sits close to me and puts a hand on my leg again.

I sigh as I look through the menu. "What was it you wanted to talk about?"

"I want to move in with you."

"No."

"That's it? No discussion."

"Yup."

She looks at her menu. "I want the crispy cod with chips."

I nod.

She says, "You keep telling me to move out of Eric's house. To get away from him, but I don't have anywhere to go. Except your place."

"You must have someone. A friend?"

"Nope."

"Then get a job and get your own place."

"I can't do that."

"Why?"

She looks away.

The waitress arrives. I order our meals and ice tea.

"I don't want ice tea," says Becky. "I want a glass of wine."

"Blush or White?" asks the waitress. She is blond and pretty. Somewhere in her forties. Her eyes are light brown. They darken slightly as they take a hold of Becky.

"What brand is it?"

"It's on the menu. Sutters I believe."

I scratch my forehead and toss Becky a glance that tells her to knock it off.

She squeezes my leg and pouts. "White will do I guess."

The waitress snatches up our menus and swings away.

"Why do you have to do that?" I ask.

"What?"

"Draw attention to us."

She grins. "Cause the waitress was jealous of me, and I wanted to rub it in a little."

"She looked tired and irritated to me."

"You didn't notice how she looked at you?"

"No."

Becky giggles. "You're so naïve, Matt."

I shake my head at her.

An hour later I'm driving Becky back to her car in the parking lot of the mall. She is under the influence of three glasses of wine, and hanging all over me. She puts her hands where they shouldn't be, and I gently push them away.

She kisses my ear and whispers, "I want to go home with you."

I shake my head.

"Please."

"I can't, Becky. Never again."

She pouts.

"I'm sorry," I say. "But I have to live with myself."

She scoots over and folds her arms and stares straight ahead. After a few moments, she says, "I wish I'd never met you."

I agree, but I don't say it. I ask, "Your age, you had to have had a job before. Why can't you get one now?"

"I don't want to talk about it," she replies.

I sigh, and we are quiet the rest of the way back to her car. It is nine-thirty when I idle up next to it. The parking lot is fairly empty now as stores are beginning to close.

Becky opens her door and says, "See you tomorrow night?"

"Let's wait till Thursday," I suggest.

Becky hesitates.

I watch her in the dim spray of caramel light that shines from the poles scattered across the lot. She shrugs slowly.

"That ok?" I ask.

"Guess so," she says and climbs out.

I wait until she drives away before I head for home. I breathe as though I'm pushing out a big lump of thick black air from my chest. I've seen Becky nearly every night since I became a hero. I need a break. I feel she is getting to me, weakening me, and I'm eventually going to give into her.

I don't want her to get hurt, but I also don't want to feel guilty about my relationship with her anymore.

Once was enough.

I roll down my window and smell the rush of wet night air.

I think about Pam as I drive. I think she would understand what I'm going through, and she would still love me.

Chapter Four

Nights are tough.

After I retired, Pam and I took to staying up late, but we never watched late night TV. I couldn't tell you wants on television after ten. Pam and I used to read books or talk, or just spend quiet time together. Sometimes Pam would sit in my lap and we'd simply hold each other.

I stare at my hands and the loneliness tears away inside me as I think about Pam and watch her die all over again.

She died in my arms.

That was how she wanted to go. I was the last thing she wanted to see.

The mean spirit sliding away into tears.

She reached up and touched them. She tried to smile.

I rise from my chair and fetch a beer from the fridge. I'd stopped reading when Pam died. I'm wondering if I shouldn't take it up again. I was reading a series of crime novels. I'd enjoyed the pace and tone of them. The sex was hinted at, and the violence was mild. I seemed able to relate to the villains as well as the hero. I don't know why, but it made the books more enjoyable.

I was half way through number eight when I'd stopped reading. The book was tucked away on the book case that stood next to Pam's desk. Her blank computer screen and keyboard are still on the desk top, positioned directly in front of her office chair.

Funny how I knew exactly where the book was. Funny how when I pulled it from the shelf and began to read from where I'd left off, it was as though I'd never put it down.

By midnight I'm on my third beer and a hundred pages deeper into the book. I rise and set it down on the computer desk.

Time for bed, but there is one more thing I have to do first.

I climb the stairs and enter the guest bedroom. It faces the street. I stand at the window and wait for him.

I don't have to wait very long.

He arrives shortly after midnight in a grey, older model Tahoe.

He has brought friends tonight, three of them.

Becky's man has recruited some help, and he is suddenly braver.

He doesn't just drive by this time. He stops and stares at my house.

His name is Eric. He is thirty-five, tall and thin and dark. He wears a black baseball cap turned around backward. He sips on a beer and puffs on a cigarette while he stares at my house.

I know he stays hyped up on Meth.

I know he works a swing shift at a welding shop down on the tide flats.

He knows that I've been with Becky.

He knows that I will beat the shit out of him if he ever gets rough with her again.

We both know what happened at the local corner store, and that I am not a hero.

I'm watching him through the curtains. The room is dark. He can't see me, but I can see him in a patch of street light the color of butter.

And he knows I'm watching him. He knows I'm waiting for him to make a move.

A smile breaks the dark lines of his handsome face. He tosses his cigarette into my front yard. He guzzles the rest of his beer and heaves the empty bottle up on my front porch. It lands with a thud and bounces around before rolling to a stop against my front door.

He flips me a bird and drives off.

I know he is not afraid of me. I know that the only thing holding him back is getting caught. He can't afford any more trouble with the police. He needs a plan. He needs to do this right.

I turn from the window, and think about the day I met Becky.

The day my problems started.

—⟋⟍—

It was the last week of August and it was raining.

I was depressed and lonely. I decided to get drunk, but I had only two beers left in the fridge. I drank them and they did little to ease the pain. I needed more, I always do when I'm fighting depression.

I looked around for my truck keys, but couldn't find them.

So I slipped into my Carhart jacket and walked to the local corner store. It was just over the rail road tracks, only a couple blocks away. Not a long walk, just long enough to get good and wet. The mood I was in, I didn't care.

As I went along the street, I thought about Pam and how miserable my life was without her. Our love was deep. I cared about what she thought of me and I still do. I wanted to take care of her, to please her, and I felt guilty about what I was doing, but I hoped she'd understand.

I waved at the owner of the store as I went through the door, and he waved back at me.

I shook the rain from my sleeves as I moved past the aisles of canned food and dry goods. Warm air touched my face. I walked all the way to the very end, where the coolers stood against the back wall, and I turned left.

An attractive woman in tight jeans and a yellow sweater was leaning into the wine cooler. She was searching through the cheap stuff, and blocking my way with her large beautiful butt. I could have waited for her to finish, or I could have back tracked and walked around to the other side. But I decided to squeeze by her, and that decision changed everything. I turned sideways, pressed my back against a row of canned soup, and eased my way into the gap. The woman suddenly backed up, right into my arms.

She squealed.

"Oops, I'm sorry," I sighed.

"It's okay, my fault," she said.

We tossed each other a quick smile. Our eyes caught briefly.

She giggled and returned to her search of the wine section.

I moved over and opened the beer cooler. I grabbed a half rack of Icehouse, and I took the back aisle to the sales counter. When Pam was alive I used to drink the more expensive micro-brews. I drank a lot less then, and could afford it. Now, I'd acquired a taste for the cheaper, high octane stuff. It got me where I wanted to go in a hurry, and I didn't give a shit how it tasted along the way.

This place is owned by a gentleman who claims he is from South Vietnam. He calls himself Duck or something like that. He has that pleasant Vietnamese nature which seems familiar to me. His smile reaches all the way up into his muddy brown eyes. We've known each other long enough to exchange a few pleasantries while I bought the beer. In the meantime, the attractive woman had found a bottle of Boons Farm, and she came up behind me.

I told Duck to take it easy, and he said for me to do the same. As I turned, I glanced at the woman, and she smiled again.

I thought about the dark green of her eyes and the nice shape of her butt as I walked out into the rain which had increased in velocity while I'd been in the store.

So I popped up the collar on my Carhart jacket as I started for home. I had my beer- anodyne, and this was a good day to pound a few nails into my depression. I resumed my thoughts about Pam and my miserable life without her, and I was a hundred yards from the store when the woman from the wine cooler suddenly pulled to the curb in a light blue Toyota sedan.

She waved for me to climb in.

I stood and stared at her for a moment, and then for the life of me I don't know why, but I did. I could have nearly tossed a rock into my back yard.

I set the half rack on the floor between my feet.

She reached over to shake my hand.

"Becky Somers," she said.

I shook her hand. It was soft and dry.

"Matt Conner."

We studied each other for a moment and it didn't feel awkward.

The rain pounded down on the hood and the roof of her Toyota. A car hissed by out on the street. I heard the song, "California Dreaming," by The Mommas and The Papas coming from her stereo.

"I like the music of the sixties and seventies," she said.

I nodded.

She smelled of perfume and cosmetics.

I smelled of beer and wet clothing.

"Well," she said. "How do I find your place?"

"Take the next left. Go over the rail road tracks. Turn left on the first street over and I'm the third house down."

'You live on Meeker?"

"Yup."

"I love those old houses."

I looked out the window at the rain.

"I really do," she added.

I nodded.

She pulled from the curb. We didn't talk while she drove me home. It was maybe a half a minute drive. She kept both hands on the wheel and looked straight ahead. When she pulled over out front of my home, I told her thanks and reached for the handle on my half rack.

"You're alone," she said as she gazed at my house.

I was a little startled, but I recovered quickly. "Yea, guess you could say that."

"Why don't you invite me in?"

I shrugged.

"Why would I do that?"

She cleared her throat.

"I've always loved these old houses on Meeker. I'd love to see what it's like on the inside of one. I won't stay long. I won't bother you."

I couldn't think of a good reason not to let her see the inside of my house. Why not? She seemed like a nice person. I liked her boldness. I liked her green eyes. I noticed a touch of teal in them when the light was just right. I also liked the way she smelled and moved, and I'd be paying her back for the ride.

"I guess I could show you around," I rasped.

She laid a smile on me that could've melted a chunk of glacier ice. We climbed out and rushed through the rain to the cover of my front porch.

I let us in, and noticed that she'd stuffed the bottle of wine into her big leather purse. She waited at the front door while I went to the kitchen and put the half rack into the fridge. I removed my jacket and hung it up in the coat closet off the little hallway on my way back into the great room.

"We'll start upstairs," I said.

"I like it already," she replied.

I showed her all the rooms. I'm not a messy person. I had nothing to hide or be embarrassed of. The layout of my house was small and simple. Two bedrooms and a full bath upstairs, a kitchen, dining room, guest bathroom and great room downstairs. It took maybe twenty minutes to show it all to her, and though she didn't make any comments, I could tell by the look in her eyes she was impressed.

Those eyes with the touch of teal in them, and something else.

We finished the tour in the great room, back at the front door.

"Thank you," she said.

"You're welcome, and thank you again for the ride."

She smiled.

I smiled.

"Would you like me to stay a little while?" she asked.

"Why would you want to do that?"

"Women in their thirties are attracted to men in their fifties."

"I'm sixty-two," I said. "And you can't be too far into your thirties."

She laughed. "You look younger. Mid fifties, maybe."

"Yea, I've heard that before."

She glanced away.

"As pretty as you are," I said. "You have someone more your own age."

"He's mean to me."

"Leave him."

She sighed, "He wasn't always. I keep hoping he'll be nice again like he was when I first moved in with him."

I shrugged. "Where is he now, at work?"

"No. He works the swing shift at a fab shop down on the tide flats. He should be sleeping, but he's out looking for more crank. He's hung up on that stuff. He wasn't when I met him. He's a different person now."

"Don't you have anyone to turn to? Your parents. A brother or sister. Friends?"

She shook her head.

"So you bought a bottle of wine to take home and drink and sleep it off and hope things are better when you wake up."

She blushed. "Pretty much, yea."

I rubbed my eyes.

"What about you?" she asked.

I thought about it for a moment, and then I said, "Yea. Pretty much I guess. Lost my wife about a year ago and it still hurts, and I try to deal with it."

"Well?"

We sat on the couch.

She drank her wine.

I drank my beer.

We didn't have to talk to feel comfortable. It was easy, not odd.

I turned on the TV, found an old beach party movie from the sixties, and after a while, she scooted in close to me and I noticed a small bruise around her right eye that she'd tried to cover with makeup. I wanted to ask her about it, but she started kissing me, and I liked the way she tasted. Next thing you know, I'm feeling of her butt and she's playing with the hair on my chest.

I don't believe either of us really intended for it to go as far as it did. And at the one point where we knew it was our last chance to stop it, we didn't. I gave in to desire, and she gave in to something I will never understand.

She wore small, simple things under her clothes. She was soft and she smelled nice. It was easy to want her.

I am hairy, scarred up, tough and durable. I also have a small roll of chub hanging over my belt. I have brown eyes and brown hair that has way more salt than pepper in it. I don't know what she saw in me.

We did it right there on the couch. Both of us were eager. It didn't take long for either of us to reach that special moment. I liked the sounds she made, but I knew in my heart this was wrong.

All wrong.

Pam would not approve.

A half hour later we were dressed and standing at the front door.

She didn't appear the least bit embarrassed. She seemed happy.

I was bothered by all of it, and I'd noticed two more bruises on her. One on her tummy, and another on her shoulder. I had to ask about them.

"Who gave you those bruises? Does your man beat you?"

She sighed and glanced down at her shoes.

"You need to leave him, Becky."

"I have no place to go," she said as she looked at me with slivers of teal sliding through her eyes.

I felt as though I had just committed a sin that would be hard to forgive. I wanted to distance myself from it, but I couldn't get away.

"There has to be someone," I said.

She searched my eyes for a moment. "Can I see you again?"

"No," I answered too quickly.

She tilted her head to the side and gazed at me out the dark green corners of her eyes. "You sure about that."

I nodded slowly.

———

That was how it started and how it should have ended, but it didn't end there.

Not even close.

Chapter Five

I'm up at seven. I start some coffee, and while it brews I step out on the front porch and remove the beer bottle. When Pam was alive, we received a morning paper from Tacoma. Pam worked the crossword puzzles while I read the sports section. Sometimes we'd browse through the news stories and the editorials. They were always slanted from the left, but still informative, and we had Fox News to hear the other side of it anyway.

I still watch Fox and Friends, but it's not the same without Pam.

She made the best coffee I've ever had. She ground the beans fresh every morning, and slow brewed them. To every cup she added just the right amount of heated condensed milk and brown sugar. We'd sit on the couch with our first cup. She'd work her cross word puzzles and I'd browse through the sports section while Fox and Friends filled us in on the world news.

It never mattered what was going on.

It was always peaceful in our living room.

I miss Pam so much it hurts all the way into my bones at times.

I cancelled the paper after she died. When they asked me why, I told them they were too liberal in their views. You think that bothered them?

I look outside and see grey clouds and fog.

I feel depressed and restless.

Maybe I'll look for a pair of shoes today. Maybe I won't.

A while later, I'm still thinking about Pam and shoes when Becky calls.

"Hey, Matt, how bout we meet for lunch today instead of waiting for dinner."

"I thought we agreed to wait till Thursday," I say. "Something change?"

"Sort of, yea."

I wait her out.

"I'm worried about Eric," she says. "He's up to something. He's got some new friends. Druggies. He's hanging out with them. They scare me."

I remember that Eric had company on his drive-by last night, but I'm thinking so what, he's still a chicken-shit, and they probably are too.

"Has Eric touched you?" I ask.

"No."

"Have his new friends touched you?"

"No."

"Then why are you scared, Becky?" I bark.

She's quiet.

I feel bad for raising my voice, but I'm tired of feeling strapped with her problems.

She finally says, "I'm scared because I don't have anyone except you, Matt."

I scratch my forehead and think about the situation. If I don't help her and she gets hurt, it will be my fault. She could be over reacting, but what if she isn't. I decide to tell her something I really don't want to. "On my back porch," I say, "there is a key under a flower pot. If things...."

"I love you, Matt," she says and hangs up.

I know I've just made a mistake by letting her know about the key, but I'm not going to turn my back on a woman in distress.

There are very few things left in this world that I care about. My 1973 Mustang in the detached garage is one of them, and Pam's wedding ring in her jewelry box upstairs in the bedroom is another. Right off hand I can't think of much else, but there are things in life that I've never been able to tolerate, and I'm not going to start now.

I can't, because to do so would be to start dying, and I'm not ready to do that just yet. I still believe in the culture I grew up in. I still believe in that culture's divine order: God, family, guns and country. I believe this order is what made America work. I also believe she has strayed away from it, and that is what is killing her.

To tolerate things that are wrong is to die inside.

I'm no saint, but I know right from wrong.

I walk on out to the detached garage, turn on the radio and pick up a nine-sixteenths box end wrench. They are playing "Tiny Dancer" by Elton John and I remember the time Pam and I had a '71 Chevy El Camino that was to light in the rear end for the horsepower under the hood.

We hadn't been married a year yet. This was before I started rough necking in Alaska. I was working on a bridge building crew in Tacoma. I had weekends off, and every Sunday afternoon, we went out for a drive. We were out by Eatonville on a small dirt road that shouldered a tiny lake where people had built cabins.

It wasn't raining when we left home, but it was by the time we reached the small lake, and true to its nature, the El Camino lost traction and slid us into a ditch.

I climbed out and cussed and stomped around until I was good and wet, and then I climbed back inside. I remember how heavy and dark the world felt in the pounding rain. I remember the anger pushing hard against my chest, and then Pam reached out and touched my face. Suddenly, it all fell away from me. I was aware of nothing else in the whole world except her.

The smell of her hair. The look in her eyes. The smile on her lips.

The sun was shining somewhere.

She could do that.

She was special.

By the time a jeep load of kids drove up, we had the windows fogged over.

The driver shouted, "Hey, mister, you wanna pull?"

I cracked my window and said, "Yea, can you give me a minute."

He nodded and grinned at his buddies. There were four of them in the jeep. Teenagers, high school, by the looks of them.

I remember how Pam blushed and giggled. She had her jeans and panties pulled down and gathered on one leg. I had my shirt off and my paints down to my thighs.

It took us a few minutes to be presentable.

I see us now, together, sharing a moment in time that we will never have again, and I fight off the tears.

I'm back in the house by eleven. I shower and shave and think about Pam, and I'm wondering if I'll ever stop hurting. I also wonder if I ever want to.

I never want to let go of what Pam and I had, but I know that I have to move on with my life. I know she would want me to.

Sometimes I feel as though I'm testing the temperature of the water in a pond, but I'm afraid it might be just right. So I tell myself it's too cold or too hot to jump in. That way I'm safe to stay right where I'm at.

In my comfort zone the temperature is not perfect anymore, but it's tolerable, and I'm doing okay.

Long as I have my memories, my beer, my radio and my old car, it's okay.

I'm good with it, anyway, and I don't care what others think.

I have something to do this afternoon. It's something I'd stopped doing right after Pam died, but I'd taken it up again a couple months ago.

I lock up my house and fire up my Chevy truck. I take the 512 into South Tacoma. I think about Pam as I drive. She'd encouraged me to join a veteran's group. She'd thought it would be good for me.

She was right, because in the early seventies the only help a Vietnam veteran could get was from other veterans. Through the years I've been a member of several groups.

Some of them were good for me, and some not so good. I've always remained skeptical of making friends, but I've never doubted the results of a total effort a group can conjure up.

Hearing others tell you what they suffer doesn't make your suffering any easier, but it helps you deal with it.

It worked for me anyway.

That was a long time ago. What I have now is something else. I'm not sure what to call it.

Chapter Six

We meet up at a restaurant in South Tacoma every Wednesday.

There used to be five of us, but now there are only three. Jimmy died of cancer, and Ken disappeared.

When Jimmy died we went to his funeral.

When Ken disappeared, we drove to his apartment out on the east end of town. His landlord let us in. The place was neat and tidy.

His landlord told us he'd not seen Ken for a while, and the rent was way overdue. He wanted to know what he should do with his things. Ken didn't have much--some clothing in the closet, food in the fridge and a few personal items in the bathroom.

We told him we didn't know what he should do.

The three of us eat lunch, drink beer and talk. We don't talk about Ken or Jimmy, and we don't talk about Vietnam anymore. We talk about anything that comes to mind, but never about our war, Ken or Jimmy.

Steve starts telling us about how he is tired of those Wounded Warrior commercials and all the other special treatment they give to veterans now a days. "What did we get," he says. "They were ashamed of us. They acted as though we lost the war, instead of the politicians. They hand-cuffed us and then wanted to know why we couldn't tie our shoes."

Clark shakes his head. "They learned from the mistakes they made with us, I guess. I feel just as sorry for those crippled vets coming home from the Middle East as I did about our guys. I'm glad to see..."

"Uh bull," snaps Steve. His face and bald head redden as his blood pressure rises. He goes off on America and I stop listening.

I gaze around the restaurant. The lunch crowd has thinned out. Only a few late arrivals remain. This place is on South Tacoma Way. It is small and clean and comes with a view of traffic. The food is greasy, and the beer is cold.

Steve is telling us how America has become a garbage can through the means of diversity and political correctness. We're not a melding pot, we're a trash can, and now the country is run by a bunch of liberals who want us to believe they really give a rat's ass about the people who sacrificed their blood and tears to keep us free.

Clark is drinking his beer and shaking his head.

I notice an attractive woman, in her thirties, seated with a man in his fifties. They are enjoying an after meal drink. They are holding hands across the table. He is all tanned up and looks to be a body builder. She is all dolled up and looks to a model. I figure he got his tan on some warm beach, and he made his muscles in a gym. I can understand her attraction to him.

In contrast, my tan comes from working out in the sun. It is what people call a farmer's tan, arms, face and neck. And my muscles were made from working hard on bridges and drilling rigs. I'm not in to bad of shape. After I retired, Pam kept me on a healthy diet, and I've always been active. But compared to the gentleman at the other table, it's no contest.

I think about Becky, and our relationship. I believe she is attracted to me for the wrong reasons, and it's not right.

Steve interrupts my thoughts. "Matt, what do you think of the man in the Whitehouse?"

"I don't know," I say. "I didn't vote for him, and I don't give him much thought."

"Are you shitting me?"

I shake my head. "I'll put it this way. I'm not as concerned about him as I am the people who twice elected him, but I can't do anything about either of them, so I don't really care anymore."

Clark, who is a little on the heavy side and has a huge grey mustache, smiles and says, "Matt's got the right attitude. If you can't change it, why bother with it."

"We got screwed," says Steve as he turns red enough to blow an o-ring. He is on the thin side of skinny, and his eyes are the color of dry oak leaves. "The guy's not even an American citizen. He applied for foreign aid when he went to college."

Clark works his mustache for a moment, and looks at me.

I shrug. Because without Pam, I really don't give a shit anymore. This country can elect Donald Duck for president and I wouldn't care.

I look at it this way: There is no difference between voting for someone because of his skin color, and not voting for him because of it.

If you think there is, you're an idiot who probably shouldn't have the right to vote anyway.

That's my take on it.

Steve cuts into my thoughts again, "You know the last two elections were rigged, right?"

Clark says, "Both of them?"

"You bet, and it got covered up."

Clark works his mustache and looks at me.

I ask, "Do you think GW beat Gore fair and square?"

"Yes, I do," replies Steve. "I think the democrats were up to foul play in Florida, and it back fired on them."

Clark says, "I saw a program on Nova that says otherwise."

Steve shakes his head. "Nova is liberal. It don't count."

Clark's about to argue that, but I stop him with, "It's getting late. I need to get home and take care of some stuff."

I push my plate away and down the reminder of my second beer.

Steve looks at his watch. "Man you are right. It's after three."

Clark tosses me a comical nod. We both know what happens when you argue with Steve.

We rise and throw on our coats and step outside. We shake hands and tell each other to take care, see you next week.

On my drive home, I think about the hanging chads in Florida. I don't know who is right about what happened down there. Pam and I voted for Bush and we were glad he won. I don't recall either of us being too concerned about whether it was completely fair or not, and I decide I still don't care. My whole point with the question was that the losing side always cries foul play, don't they?

It's the American way, I guess.

I reach home by four, and in the lonely quietness of my house, I feel comfortable.

Faye calls while I'm removing my jacket.

"Hello, Matt. How about some dinner?" she asks.

"Not tonight," I say. "But thanks for the offer."

"Are you feeling okay?"

"I'm fine. A little tired."

"How was lunch with your friends?"

I know she means well, but I feel she's prying a little. "It was typical," I say, and then I add, "I'm a little bored at times."

She sighs.

"I'll talk to you later, maybe. I have something I need to do right now."

"Okay, Matt. Didn't mean to hold you up. If you change your mind, dinner is at six."

We hang up. I rush to the bathroom and pee out the two beers I'd had with lunch. Then I go upstairs and change into my work jeans and a flannel shirt. I feel like tinkering with the Mustang for a while this evening. I don't feel like talking. If Faye thinks I'm rude, she'll have to live with it.

I go out the back door and down the porch steps. I start off across the lawn toward the detached garage, but my neighbor, Dick Holly, calls to me over the fence. He lives on the opposite side of me from Faye Evans. He is a realtor, and his wife, Silvia, is a loan officer at a local bank.

Dick and Silvia have always been good neighbors. When Pam was alive we used to cook out with them once in a while on warm summer evenings. When Pam became sick they were always there to help out. Silvia brought food over all the time, and Dick made his son mow my lawn.

Dick and Silvia are Democrats, but I've never held that against them. Pam encouraged me to look for the good things in people no matter what their political beliefs were, and there are a lot of good things in Dick and Silvia.

Dick has always liked to bond a little with me over the fence. It's an old male thing where you stand on your property and talk to your neighbor while he stands on his. It's harmless and traditional, and if you are under forty you probably don't have a clue what I'm talking about.

Dick says, "How's Matt the hero doing?"

I angle over to the fence and lean on my side of it.

"I'm not much of a hero, Dick," I say with a grin.

He smiles. "A man does a little brown nosing to get a promotion and they call him an ass kisser. A man stops a woman from getting beat up in the local corner store and they call him a hero."

I glance off toward the river. A train rushes by on the tracks. The air is suddenly full of warm noise and the smell of burnt diesel fumes.

We wait for the train to pass.

Dick asks, "So how you been doing?"

"Getting by. Your kids are off to college now?"

He nods. "Yup. Just me and Silva. Funny how you work hard to get the kids out of the house and then you miss them."

I glance down at the flower bed along the fence where I'm standing and I think about how badly Pam had wanted kids.

Dick clears his throat and says, "By the way, Silva told me to invite you over for lunch on Saturday afternoon."

I nod.

"I'm cooking steaks," he adds.

"Call and remind me on Saturday morning," I say. I'm already thinking of excuses.

Dick smiles. "Well I better run. Let you go work on the old girl in the garage. How's she coming? Going to fire her up soon?"

"Maybe," I rasp. I grin and turn and walk to the garage.

I unlock the door with a key and switch on a light. I turn on the radio and hear classic rock at a low volume. I don't like my music loud.

I grab a three-eighths box end wrench and lean into the engine compartment.

Pam and I had bought the Mach One about a year before I retired. We found it parked on a vacant lot with a for sale sign in the window. It didn't run, and two tires were flat. We paid cash for it, hired a tow truck and brought her home. I've worked on her since the moment she touched down in my garage. She's in far better shape now. I've rebuilt the engine, transmission and rear-end. She's all cleaned up and has chrome rims and new tires on her. I know that the Mach Ones were never the kings of the road like the Shelby Cobras were, but the Mach Ones were a damn nice ride in their day. This one has the Cleveland 351 in it. I put a four barrel Holley on her and straight dual exhaust with glass packed mufflers. She'll grab about 385 foot pounds of torque from her 300 horses.

I know that's not great, but I'm good with it.

I'm not into the Chevy versus Ford verses Dodge bullshit. I know people who are, and that's fine, whatever fires their boilers. As for me, in the last forty years I've owned all three, and I've always had an equal amount of good and bad luck with them.

If I had the money and the room in my garage, I'd have a '68 Camaro and a '70 Charger parked on each side of the Mustang. That's how I feel about it, and I'll tell you something else, I wouldn't own a foreign automobile even if you put my tongue in a vise. I don't care how good they are. Drive what you want to drive, just don't complain to me about jobs going overseas.

As I start to work I feel better. The music takes me back to the seventies, when life was a lot simpler and I see Pam in a pair of shorts bringing me a cold beer on a hot afternoon. Her legs are long and slender and white. She has a nice sway to her hips. She is smiling. The blue in her eyes is as soft as powder.

I'm in no hurry to finish the Mustang. Matter of fact, I never want to be finished tinkering with it. My world spins in the right direction when I'm working on this old car. Why would I want it to stop? I have good memories of the seventies. Why would I want them to ever end?

Chapter Seven

The evening slips away.

    I skip dinner because I can't decide what to microwave tonight. If I'm losing weight, I don't care. I can remember when plump was considered healthy, and skinny was considered unhealthy. That was a long time ago. The world has changed and thinking about it makes me feel depressed and lonely again.

I long to be with Pam. I never dreamed that losing her would hurt this much. At times, I wonder if I shouldn't try going back to work, but what would I do, push carts at Wal-Mart? I'm old and I'm white, unfortunately, that's the two categories where job discrimination is still legal. The government says it isn't, but the next time you're at Wal-Mart, do the math.

By eight I'm sitting in my easy chair. I am drinking a beer and watching an old Clint Eastwood western on TV. "Joe Kid."

Back in the Seventies there used to be some good sitcoms on evening television. Pam and I enjoyed several of them. The story lines were simple and we could relate to the characters. But somewhere along the way into the Twenty-first Century, sitcoms changed to accommodate their audiences. Pam and I stopped watching them years ago. I couldn't even tell you what's on anymore.

My loss, I guess, but I'll settle for Clint Eastwood any day, and I'm engrossed when I suddenly realize that I'm not alone.

Becky uses the key under the flower pot on the back porch and comes waltzing in all dolled up. She is wearing a yellow skirt and a white cotton sweater. She says to me, "Don't worry. I parked my car a block away. No one saw me."

I'm startled as I rise from my chair.

She moves back into the hallway and explains. "I'm worried about his three friends. I don't like the way they look at me. I'm afraid, Matt. I don't understand Eric anymore. I don't know what he's up to. He didn't sleep at all today. Came home in time to shower and grab the lunch I packed for him. Never said a word to me."

I close my eyes and rub my forehead. I feel sorry for her. I don't want her to be afraid of me. I shrug and say, "It's okay, Becky. I'm not upset with you. I'm angry with the situation."

"I'm sorry to intrude, but…."

"I know. You startled me a little, that's all."

"I put the key back under the pot," she says as she walks to the couch and sits down. She crosses her legs and pulls a bottle of Boons Farm from her giant leather purse.

I turn off the television. I walk over to the couch and sit down on the edge of the coffee table in front of Becky.

She is removing the cap from the wine bottle.

I watch her take a drink. I watch her neck work as she swallows the wine. I stare at her wet pink lips. I notice she is wearing ear rings that are little ruby hearts dangling from tiny gold chains. I smell her perfume and her hair.

"Becky," I say. "I don't know if I can help you anymore. I'm an old man who should have known better than to get involved with you to begin with. It is as much my fault as it is yours. But it can't--we can't go on like this. We have to do something about Eric. Are you sure you have no one else to turn to."

"Positive," she says. She lowers the wine bottle to her lap and holds it with both hands. Her lips are thick and shiny. Her green eyes are liquid smooth with the strips of teal in them.

I glance at her ankles. They have a nice shape to them. I'm aroused, but I try not to let it show. I close my eyes again and try to think this through.

Becky says, "I want to be with you, Matt. You are my lover. And you are my hero."

I shake my head. "We are not lovers, and you know I'm no hero."

She acts as though she doesn't hear me. She drinks more wine and says, "I need you. You're all I have."

I watch her and want her, and feel as though there are rusty nails poking me in the chest.

Becky moves and her skirt slides up her thighs a little. I wonder if she is allowing this to happen. Has she read me?

I stand up and walk into the kitchen. I check the lock on the back door, and then I open the fridge. I don't want another beer, but I take one anyway.

At midnight I am standing at the window in the guest bedroom. I wait for Eric, and he arrives on time. His friends are with him. They stop where my truck is parked in its space at the curb. They sit there a moment and talk before they toss a couple of empty beer bottles into the bed. I hear them land with a clunk. I hear them roll around and thump against the back of the cab. Eric and his friends laugh. They look up at me and nod their heads as they drive off slowly.

I go down stairs, walk through the house and check the door locks again. I open the coat closet and take down my old Dan Wesson .357 magnum pistol. I also have a Ruger .22 mag., and a twelve gauge shotgun, but I'm most comfortable with the Dan Wesson.

I take the gun into the kitchen. I empty it, clean it and reload it. I hold it up to the light. It feels heavy and awkward in my hand. It smells of gun oil and old bullets. It has walnut grips and a five inch barrel on it. It's been years since I've fired the gun, but I am certain it still works.

It is nearly three am before I turn out the lights and climb the stairs.

Becky is standing at Pam's night stand with her back to me. She is wearing a white bikini brief and nothing else. Her hair hangs down her back in sleep tangles. She's opened the lid on Pam's musical jewelry box. It plays the song "You've got a Friend" by Carol King.

When I hear it, I suddenly feel as though someone suddenly punches me in the heart. My voice drops an octave as I say, "Please shut the lid."

She closes it gently and stares at it in the silence.

"Thanks," I rasp.

"Sorry," she whispers.

I nod as I stare at the small of her back.

"The one ring in there with the diamond on it. Was that her wedding ring?"

"Yea," I say. "She removed it the day she died. Wants me to bring it along when I go to her."

Becky turns to me. The yellow glow of the lamp light plays on her bare breasts. "You really miss her, don't you," she says.

"I guess so," I say.

She smiles and crawls back into bed.

I stare at her as I undress.

I think it's odd that Becky never met Pam, and she's never asked me about her, yet she seems to have known her. It's as though the two times she's been in my house were all she needed to connect. Or maybe it's deeper. Maybe it's a feeling of presences. A female thing.

I don't know or understand.

I only know that it's wrong for me to sleep with Becky, and yet I do.

Chapter Eight

I've heard that in a sexual relationship, the second time is always better than the first. Maybe that's because you are more relaxed and you know more about each other. I remember what it was like with Pam. We were madly in love, and eager to please one another.

The second time with Becky was everything it shouldn't have been. My head is spinning slightly when I wake at seven to the smell of brewing coffee.

My first thought is of wishing I were young enough to be her man. My second is of how foolish that sounds. My relationship with her is wrong, and it has to end.

I'm dumbfounded when I go down stairs and find the pot of coffee she brewed for me. She'd found the beans in the fridge. She'd ground them and made the coffee. She has condensed milk and brown sugar sitting out on the counter next to my favorite blue cup.

How in hell did she know these things?

Becky is dressed. She sits at the table with her legs crossed. She smiles at me. She lifts a cup of coffee and sips.

I close my eyes and rub my forehead. I feel cat claws gripping my heart. "Becky," I rasp. "I can't do this."

"What's wrong?"

"I can't have this relationship with you. It's not right."

"Have a cup of coffee. Maybe you'll feel better," she says.

"I want you to leave."

She sips and stares at me.

"I don't mean to be rude. Last night was good, but I need to be alone and think about this."

"What's to think about?" she asks.

I shake my head at her.

She sets the coffee cup down and rises. She picks up her giant leather purse and moves in close to me. I can smell her sleep breath and perfume. She stares into my eyes and then plants a big kiss on my mouth, gently biting my bottom lip as she pulls away.

She turns and leaves through the back door.

I follow her out onto the porch. I watch her cross the yard and turn right at the alley. She disappears behind my detached garage.

I remove the key from under the flower pot. Once back inside, I dump out the coffee she'd made for me. I grind and start a fresh pot.

While the coffee brews I go out and remove the beer bottles from the bed of my truck. I put them in the trash can under my sink. A few minutes later I'm seated at the kitchen table, sipping on my first cup and wondering if I shouldn't call my little brother, Dean, in Portland and see if he'd like some company.

I have not talked to him since Pam's funeral. He came up for it. He's always been a good brother. We were very close before I went to Vietnam.

Dean and I were raised along the soggy shores on the south end of Puget Sound. Our father was a used car salesman who loved to fish, and our mother was an art teacher who loved to paint the big houses of the rich people who lived in the hills above the shoreline.

We never owned a house.

We had to rent them because Dad moved us around a lot. He worked the dealerships along Pacific Highway all the way from the south end of Seattle to Olympia. Mom never complained. She always had her brushes and her canvas. She taught art at the Highline Community College, she drove to school from whatever house we called home.

Dad died when I was thirteen and Dean was twelve. He died suddenly and he left us with nothing. We don't talk about him or the way he died.

We moved on with our lives.

We had to.

Mom never remarried, and I do not remember her having much of a social life. She worked all the time. She moved us into an apartment in Midway, and when she wasn't teaching art, she was washing dishes at a greasy spoon.

She counted on me to take care of Dean, and I gladly did so. Dean was easy to look after. Hell, he was always reading a book or working a puzzle.

I was the one probably needed looking after. I liked to fight a little. I liked drinking beer and chasing girls and driving hotrods.

Mom said that I lived life with one foot on a banana peel and the other one on the gas pedal. I joined the Army right out of high school because it was highly suggested that I do so by a juvenile judge.

Mom past away from cancer while I was in Vietnam.

Dean waited until after he'd buried her to tell me. He never explained why, but knowing him, the reason would be justifiable.

He was a good person. Always level headed and easy to get along with.

I smile at the memories of him. He owns a heavy equipment company now. He lives in a big house with a view of the river, and a beautiful wife. They have three kids and four grandchildren.

I stare at the phone and think about giving him a call. I know that whether he's busy or not, he'd tell me to come down, he'd love to see me. But I feel that would be running away from my problems. I'd never done that before. I didn't want to start now.

There has to be another way to deal with Becky.

I think about the teal in her eyes right before she'd planted the kiss.

I think about last night.

Becky is making her way into my life, and she's dragging her luggage with her. If I were ten years younger, no, twenty years younger, I'd have a different attitude. But I'm not, and I don't, and I have no idea what I'm going to do about her.

I'm outside mowing my yard by nine.

It is a beautiful September day. The air has a slight chill in it, and it smells of the cottonwoods down on the Puyallup River.

Faye is out working her fall garden. She is wearing a pair of tan shorts and a blue cotton blouse. She waves at me, and I wave back. She turns and gives me the view that lets me know gravity still hasn't been to hard on her.

I look away. I finish mowing the grass, and then I trim the flower beds. I pull some weeds and rough up the soil with a garden rake.

I'm back inside my house by eleven. I'm drinking ice water and wondering what I should do about Becky, when Faye calls.

"Matt," she says. "How about lunch?"

I gaze down at the floor and try to think of a good excuse to decline. I'm drawing a blank when I glance at my shoes, and I'm suddenly hit with a what-the-hell notion. "Do you know where I can get a good pair of shoes?" I blurt.

"What?"

"A good pair of shoes. I need to buy some and I'm not sure where Pam used to get them."

She is quiet, but not for long. "Well sure I do. You want me to help you find some?"

"Yes. If you want to. I will buy you lunch where ever you'd like to eat."

"Be ready in about twenty minutes," she says.

"Make it thirty," I say. "I need a shower and a shave."

She says something I don't catch and hangs up.

I have the feeling there is a gun to my head.

I wonder why I'm doing this while I shower, and I think it's because I want to put distance between myself and my relationship with Becky. I hope hanging around with someone closer to my own age will help me do so.

That sounds good, right. And I also hope I'm not making another mistake.

The phone is ringing as I'm about to leave.

I know it is Becky, and I answer it.

"Low."

"We still meeting up at the mall tonight?"

"I'd rather not, Becky."

"Did I do something wrong this morning?"

I think about it before I say, "No, I guess I just don't feel right about our relationship."

She sighs into the phone.

I wait.

"What if Eric beats on me. He's mad about me not coming home last night. I'm scared. He's up to something, I can feel it. His friends are gross. They look at me crazy."

I say nothing.

"I don't know what to do, Matt. He is acting weird. Hanging out with his new friends and they are snorting Meth, and drinking all day. He passes out for a few hours this morning, and then he's back up. I told him I was with you last night."

I stare down at the floor.

"Please let me come over, or meet me at the mall tonight."

I think about it all for a moment. I see myself climbing into her Toyota. I see myself lusting for her as she lay on my bed with the lift of her bare breasts covered in soft room shadows.

I'm as guilty as she is for what happened, but I will not be able to live with myself if I allow it to go on this way.

"I'm sorry," I say. "I just don't think we should…."

She hangs up.

I put the phone down and stare at it.

Faye meets me at my truck. She is wearing a light grey pants suit that hugs the curves of her body. She is dolled up and smells nice and smiles at me as though we are kids out on our first date.

I open the passenger door for her and help her up onto the seat. We touch hands briefly.

"I like your truck," she says as I fire it up and pull from the curb.

I smile. My truck is a dark blue '88 Silverado 4X4 with the 5.7, 230 horsepower engine in it. I put a small lift on her, cold air intake, and dual exhaust. I like the way she sounds and runs.

Fay stares at the side of my face. "You look nice, and I like the smell of your aftershave. What's the name of it?"

"Usher," I say. "You look nice too. Want to eat lunch before we shop, or after?"

"Where are we going?"

"Tacoma."

"No need in driving that far. South Hill Mall has several shoe stores, and there are some good restaurants up on the hill as well."

"Okay."

I drive over to Meridian and swing south to the hill.

Faye talks while I drive. Actually, she sort of shouts, and I feel it's time to fess up. So I cut her off with an apology.

"I'm sorry," I say. "I have a confession to make."

She stares at the side of my face again. Her dark red lips are pursed into a tiny smile.

"I don't hear as well as I should. All those years of working on bridges and drilling rigs damaged some of my hearing, but I'm not as deaf as I've pretended to be."

"I know that," she says.

I glance at her.

She reaches over and squeezes my arm. "You are a dear darling hero, Matt."

I think about telling her the truth about that hero stuff, closing the book on it for good, but I'm not sure if this is the time or the place just yet, so I let it go.

I drive on, and she goes back to talking. It was a good fifteen minutes up the hill to the mall, and another three minutes finding a parking space, and in that amount of time, Faye told me all about her sister who lives in Yakama with three dogs and a cat and a husband who refurbishes old automobiles. I'm interested in old automobiles, so I ask her a few questions about her brother-in-law. She doesn't know that much about him and his business, but she assures me he makes good money.

The way she says it gives me the feeling good money is important to her.

We enter the mall. She takes my arm and directs me to one of several shoe stores. She seems to know what I like. Leather, three quarter high, brown lace ups in a size ten or ten and a half, depending on how the shoe is made.

I find myself staring at a choice of three different styles. I try all three pair on and select the one that fits best.

Faye nods her approval of my choice.

As I'm buying the shoes, I ask, "Where would you like to eat?"

"The Ram," she says without hesitation. "I love that place."

I nod and smile.

We return to my truck and she tells me about her brother who lives in Aberdeen with his second wife and all her children. Faye's brother is a retired Boeing engineer who had money until he divorced his first wife and married the money sponge.

I find myself enjoying Faye's company more than I'd ever imagined. I like the way she smiles and takes my arm when we walk. I like the way she sits a little close to me in the truck, and I find that I really don't mind her talking all the time. Her voice is smooth and level. She doesn't ask questions to make sure I am listening to her. She simply talks and once in a while she throws in a mild gasp to punctuate a statement.

The Ram is a sports bar. Flat screens hanging everywhere. The décor is light and airy. Blue fabric and oak wood, stone tile on the floor, and tall windows along the walls that face Meridian.

It's busy this time of day. I have to park a ways off to one side of the front entrance. I climb out, go around and help Faye down. She takes my arm and we work our way through the crowded parking lot.

Once inside, Faye asks for a booth.

A young and attractive woman notifies us that we're in luck. Faye follows her and I follow Faye. She seats us in a freshened booth that faces the corner of Meridian and

Ninety-Seventh where the Crispy Cream doughnut shop stands next to a US Bank.

A waitress appears as we are settling in. Faye orders a glass of wine and I ask for an amber ale. While we wait for our drinks, she tells me about her friends. They meet at her place once a week and play dirty bridge.

I know of them. I've seen them arrive. They all seem to have money if you go by how they dress and what they drive.

Our drinks arrive, and we order our meals.

Faye wants a salad. I want a burger and fries. The Blue Cheese burger with the steak fries, that is. I've had it before and I know it's good.

The waitress jots down our orders and swings away.

"My friends would die of envy if they could see me now," says Faye.

I toss her an awkward smile.

"Tell me if I'm pushy," she says. "I can't help myself sometimes."

"I'm not much of a prize, Faye."

She sips her wine. "You're damn handsome, Matt. I've been attracted to you for a long time. Do you mind?"

"No," I rasp. "But I want you to know I'm no hero. I simply stopped a young woman from getting pounded on. I was as scared as she was. I'm lucky the young man decided not to pursue the matter."

She smiles.

I nod, thinking that's not the whole truth, but the rest is a little embarrassing, and I'm not ready to tell her about it yet.

She asks, "Are you enjoying this, Matt?"

"Yes," I say as I look into her eyes and try to think of a way to tell her the entire situation at the corner store when I became a hero, but our food arrives and we began to eat.

Faye inquires, "Are you seeing anyone right now?"

I wonder if she's seen Becky coming or going, as I shake my head.

The waitress swings by to ask if everything is okay and if we'd like anything else. Faye wants another glass of wine, and I have a second ale.

Faye eats more of her salad, and I chew on my burger.

The drinks arrive and we both sip and gaze at each other for a moment.

I don't know what she is thinking, but I'm thinking I sort of like her more than I'd thought I ever would. Faye is desirable. Her eyes are dark and gentle. She is all woman, and by that I mean the kind of woman who takes long baths, paints her nails, spends a lot of time applying her makeup, and leaves the rough stuff to men, as it was intended to be.

I'm also thinking about how I've noticed when she has a gentleman visitor, but how I've never paid much attention to how long they've stayed.

She says, "Matt, I'm not seeing anyone either." She looks away for a moment, and then right into my eyes. "I know what the neighbors think, and I don't care. "Just because a man stops by to see me doesn't mean I'm sleeping around."

I smile and nod.

She continues with, "I get lonely and I like to have company. Is that wrong?"

I shake my head.

"I like to talk and it's nice to have someone who'll listen. Most of the men I have over are good listeners. I like to cook.

They are also good eaters." She pauses and briefly looks away again. "It's different with you, Matt. Am I making any sense?"

I think she is trying to tell me she is not a slut. I never thought she was. I never paid enough attention to draw that conclusion, I guess, and I wouldn't care much if she is. I just hope I'm able to perform if that's where this lunch leads to. That part of me still works pretty good, but I'm getting old, and Becky wore me out last night.

I take a hit form my beer and say, "I'm good with it."

Faye studies me for a moment, and then she blushes and nods.

By the time we head for home, we've both had a little too much to drink, and I'm feeling good about myself. Faye is sitting close to me and she is not talking. She looks out the window and then at her hands which are folded in her lap.

I have the feeling she is dealing with this situation. She is trying to make up her mind about what comes next.

I pull my Chevy into its little parking space at the curb which is straight across from Faye's big Lincoln. She says, "Thanks for the wonderful afternoon." and she gives me a moist peek on the cheek.

"Thank you too," I tell her as I climb out and walk around to the passenger side of the cab. I help Faye climb down and she takes my arm as I walk her to her front door.

I turn to leave and she grabs my arm. We gaze at each other for a moment, and I realize she's made up her mind. She's eager, but she has virtues to protect. This has to be done right and it has to mean something to both of us. I smile at the notion and tell her goodbye.

She plants a tiny kiss on my lips.

I turn and head for home with a feeling of heavy air in my chest.

Alone in the quiet, I think about Faye.

I like her, and in a way, I think I always have.

I remember how she used to hit on me when Pam was alive.

It was in her eyes and her actions when she was around me. She dropped subtle hints. She touched my arm when she could.

One New Year's Eve, Pam and I tossed a party for our closest neighbors. Dick and Silva, Faye, and several others we'd known for a few years were all there. Everybody was pretty well hammered by midnight, and when the cork popped, Faye grabbed me and planted a kiss on my mouth that seemed to last for five minutes or better.

I remember talking to Pam about it the next morning.

Pam never felt her marriage was threatened by Faye. She laughed about the kiss. She told me her only concern was that I might run out of air and pass out before Faye let go.

I never understood why Faye would hit on me when she was friends with Pam, and I guess I still don't.

I guess I never will, but I do understand why Pam was not worried about it. She never doubted my love for her. And she had that right, but I have to wonder now that if I have a relationship with Faye would Pam mind.

I don't think she would.

I think she is smiling.

Chapter Nine

I paid some bills in the afternoon. I still write checks, put them in an envelope and mail them. I changed the oil on my truck and washed her. I finished my day tinkering with the Mustang, and by six I'm in my chair and watching Fox News. I have a beer and a bag of Frito's chips. The chilly and cheese ones.

Becky calls at six-thirty.

"Matt," she says. "I'm scared, and I want to come over tonight."

I chew some chips and swallow.

She sighs. "I'll sleep in the guest room."

I sip my beer and say nothing, because I know that's not true.

"I'm worried, Matt. I really am. Eric and his friends are up to something."

"Makes you think that," I rasp.

"Everything. The way they act. Like they have a plan or something, and they don't want me to know about it."

I think about that for a moment.

"Probably coming for me," I say.

She's quiet, and then she asks, "Is the key under the flower pot?"

"It will be," I say.

"Did I do something wrong?"

I close my eyes. "No. You didn't."

"I don't understand what happened this morning. It's like I said the wrong thing or did something to turn you off."

"It's not you, Becky."

She starts crying.

I feel sorry for her, and I'm about to tell her to come on over when she suddenly says, "I'm sorry, Matt." And she hangs up.

I feel bad, and I think about calling her back, but I let the notion drop. I'm stuck between wanting to distance myself from her and her problems, and wanting her to do what she did to me all over again.

When it comes to sex at my age, you take what you can get. Some are lucky enough to keep the same woman that still turns them on. Becky was my first since Pam left. Pam was special, and for some reason the sex I had with Becky was also special. Sex isn't everything, I know, but oh Lord where would the world be without it.

I climb from my chair and enter the kitchen. I take the key down from the rack, go out back and put it under the flower pot. I feel as though I want Becky to come, and yet I don't.

If she comes, I know what I'm going to do--fall all over myself to get into bed with her again.

I have to face up to it. It's not right, but it's true. I love Becky for rubbing the rust off my old spark plugs, and I'm ashamed of myself for wanting more.

I read my book until mid-night. I'm ready for Becky to come waltzing in at any moment, but she doesn't. And when I climb the stairs and stand at the window in the guest bedroom, I worry about her while I wait for Eric and his pals to drive by, but they don't show.

It is nearly two before I go back down stairs and fall asleep in my chair.

Faye wakes me at nine with a phone call.

"Matt," she says. "Will you come over and take a look at a leak under my kitchen sink?"

"Guess so," I say. "I'm just waking up. Be about an hour."

"Don't eat breakfast. I'll make us a brunch."

"Okay."

We say goodbye and hang up. I climb from my recliner and walk into the kitchen. I start a pot of coffee and then I head on upstairs and take a shower. I think about Pam and feel dispirited. I think about how I'd come home from the rigs in Alaska all tensed up and restless. I remember how she used to take a shower with me and scrub my back, how she had a way of easing the tension out of me, how just being with her helped me to find peace in my heart.

All gone now, and I don't want to talk about it anymore.

I dress for the day in faded jeans and a baggy cotton pull-over shirt.

I know it is Friday in September.

I know I will go to Faye's house and fix a small leak under her kitchen sink. She will wear something that teases me a little. She will make something delicious for me to eat. She will fire me up and then gently see me to the door.

I know these things and I like them and want them.

Why not, even at my age, why not?

Faye and I come from a generation where only the catcher wore his hat backward. We were kids during the sexual revolution. I didn't buy into drugs and free love, and something tells me she didn't either. Traditional values are still important to us. The old way of doing things doesn't seem so bad. I believe Faye is following the ancient three-dates and dinner at my mother's rule. Her mother is no longer alive, so I figure she'll have to cook the dinner herself, and I also believe she is as eager as I am to get the three dates completed.

Sad, but true, the sexual revolution and free love destroyed the three date rule along with some other traditions.

And I'll tell you the truth about Pam. She did buy into drugs and free love. She slept with many strangers before she met me, but it was already to late. Free love got her liver, or snorting coke through a dollar bill with the wrong person did. The doctor told her it could have been either, but in the end it didn't really matter. I stood a good chance of being infected, but I wasn't.

Do not think I feel good or lucky about that?

I loved Pam with all my heart, and I know she loved me. We were right for each other and we never doubted it because we knew better. Not that I was ever a saint. I'd made my share of mistakes before I met Pam, and….

I don't want to talk about it anymore.

I have two cups of coffee before I cross over to Faye's house. I am fully awake and a little eager. The day is cloudy, but warm. The air smells of Puget Sound and the river. A train rushes by. A siren goes off somewhere downtown.

I wonder about Becky and hope she is okay.

Faye is wearing a pair of blue shorts that fit her tight around the butt, and flare out a little around her thighs. Her white cotton blouse shows a little cleavage. She is wearing makeup and she smells nice.

She touches my arm and gives me a peak on the cheek when she lets me in.

I follow her into the kitchen, open the doors under her sink and take a look. She has a Tupper wear bowl under a drip in the pipe where it connects to the line going through the wall. The bowl is half full.

I reach in and check the plastic fitting.

It's loose, so I tighten it.

I turn on the water and let it run. The fitting still leaks.

Faye is telling me about her friend, Wilma, who is thinking about getting married again. She is dating a man who is twenty years younger than her and is worried he might be more after her money than her companionship.

I interrupt her. "I need a pair of channel locks," I say. "I'll be right back."

She smiles and nods.

I smell what she has in the oven. I know it will be good.

I hurry over to my house. I need the key to the detached garage. It hangs on the board by the back door with the other keys.

The phone is ringing.

I pick it up in the kitchen. "Low."

"Matt. I want you to know I'm okay, but I want to see you tonight for sure."

"You home?"

"Yes."

"And Eric?"

"He's crashed out. Think he took some downers."

"And his friends?"

"I haven't seen them."

I sigh. "Maybe things will be okay, Becky."

"No," she says. "I don't trust them."

"Anything happen last night?"

"No because I wasn't here. I went somewhere. Stayed gone."

I look down at the floor and scratch my forehead. I'm thinking she went to a bar and got drunk, went home with a stranger and maybe slept with him. I'm not sure why I'm thinking this because it's not my business anyway, is it.

"Didn't Eric get mad about that?" I ask.

"He was already sleeping when I came home."

"Probably thinks you were with me."

"Will I see you tonight?"

"Becky…."

"I didn't sleep with anyone last night, if that's what you think."

I turn a little red with embarrassment, and I realize how ridicules this is getting to be.

"Okay," I sigh. "I'll meet you at the mall around seven. We'll go out to dinner."

She hangs up.

I think about her as I walk out to the detached garage and grab a pair of channel locks from my tool box. Becky's life is all messed up and it is spilling over into mine.

I need to do something about it, and soon. I feel safer meeting her at the mall and taking her out to dinner, than I do allowing her to come over, but I need to put an end to the whole thing tonight.

I head back to Faye's house and fix the leak. All it needed was a turn and a half with the channel locks.

I wash up in her guest bath room.

The bird chirps at me while I dry my hands on a towel.

Faye has baked a pastry with cherries in it. I love it and I know she is on her way to my heart through my stomach.

She serves it with coffee.

She tells me about her first husband while we eat. He was a patent lawyer. He did a lot of work for the Japanese. He took Faye to Japan one time on a business trip. She didn't like it over there, it was too crowded and it smelled of raw fish everywhere she went. She was not in love with her first husband, but he was nice to her and he left her everything when he died of stomach cancer.

In the soft grey light that floods in through the dining room window, I notice that Faye sort of resembles Joan Collins. Her hair and the lines of her face. The shape of her mouth and the color of her eyes. The way she looks at me with a slight tilt of her head.

I'm aroused, and she knows it.

I suddenly glance at my watch and see that it is nearly noon.

Faye clears her throat and rises from the table. She picks up our plates and coffee cups.

"Thank you again," she says. "For fixing the leak."

"Thanks for the brunch," I say as I stand up and head for the door.

Faye sets the plates and cups down and follows me. We stand close together. I put a hand on the door knob. She rubs my arm and bats her eyes.

"I'll see you later," I say.

She nods and gives me a full kiss on the lips. I feel like reaching down and grabbing her butt, but I hold off. It's not time. This is only date number two. I don't want to push it. I want to enjoy it.

A cool grey drizzle is falling now.

I angle across her yard and enter mine. I see a white Ford Escort parked at the curb behind my truck. I see a woman on my front porch. She looks to be in her forties. She is tall and slender. She is blond and pretty. She is wearing a brown paints suit and she is holding a note book and a camera.

"Hi," I call.

She turns to face me. "Hello. I'm looking for Matt Conner."

"That's me," I say as I reach the steps and climb up to the porch.

She reaches out a soft white hand. "Jackie Tate with the TNT."

I shake her hand and gaze into her eyes briefly. She is not one of the reporters who'd covered my hero story. But her name rings a bell. I used to take the TNT. I remember reading her column once in a while. She does human interest and follow up stories.

"What can I do for you?" I ask.

"If you have a moment," she says. "I'd like to ask you a few questions and button up a couple of loose ends."

I shake my head.

"This is a beautiful old home. Did you fix it up yourself?"

"My wife and I did."

"What year was it built?"

"1924 I believe."

"Do you mind if I take a picture of it?"

"Yes. I have nothing to add to the story. It's dead. I don't want to talk about it, and I don't want a picture of my house in the paper."

She smiles. "There are rumors. You don't want to discuss them."

"No."

She gazes at the front of my house. "I'd love to see the inside of this place. Can I at least take a peek?"

"I'm busy," I say. "I don't have the time."

She says, "Your wife past away a year ago. You must be lonely."

"I miss her very much, and she has nothing to do with the story."

She smiles at me. "Is it true you knew the girl before you rescued her?"

As a rig manager in Alaska, I was trained in the art of handling the media. The company I worked for sent all of its rig managers to a crash course on how to answer media questions in case of a major event. You never tell them you have no comment. You never say more than needed to answer a direct question.

"Not true," I say.

"You'd never met her?"

"Never."

"The store owner says you may have seen her in the store before."

I shrug.

She purses her lips. "I would really like to go inside and sit and finish this interview."

"I'm busy," I say.

"Where were you just now? Next door?"

"Yes. Fixing a plumbing leak for my neighbor."

"A woman?"

"Yes."

"Does she think of you as a hero?"

"I'm not sure."

"Oh sure you are."

"Are we finished yet?"

She sits down on the bench in front of the picture window and studies me.

I lean against one of the porch beam supports and wait her out.

She sighs and opens her note book. After reading through her notes she looks at me and asks, "How often do you shop at the little corner store?"

"Not very."

"The owner says he knows you by name."

"So."

"He says you possible knew the girl by name."

"What is her name?" I ask.

The smile slips from her face now. She realizes she is interviewing someone she cannot trap. Not yet. But she is a pro, and given time, she will trip me up. It's an art all journalists are good at.

I know this and I tell her the interview is over. "I have things to do today," I add. "And I don't have any more time for you. Goodbye."

I open my front door and enter my home. I walk straight through and out the back door onto the porch. I head out to the detached garage and the old Mustang.

Chapter Ten

I have no idea how long Jackie stays on my front porch, she is gone when I decide to have a sandwich around two in the afternoon.. I wonder if I did the right thing by not allowing her to interview me. She may think I am hiding something, but I don't care. She will write what she wants to anyway, no matter what I tell her. I can deny every rumor she spits out, and she can believe me, but still write what she wants to in order to sell papers.

That's freedom of the press.

Wonderful isn't it?

I think about Vietnam as I eat my sandwich.

I remember how the press helped us lose that war. I remember how I went over there thinking my job was to fight the spread of communism, and how I came back angry because my country chickened out on me.

The press made us look bad. They expounded on our atrocities, but said little to nothing about the communist atrocities.

The people in America were spoon fed what the media wanted them to hear. A lot of it was true, but like a sheet of plywood, every story has a smooth and a rough side to it. It's all in how you lay it. It's all in what side you expose. The majority of the South Vietnamese people wanted freedom from Communism. They wanted to live as we do in America. A liberal media and a spineless government screwed the whole thing up. Young American boys died for not a fucking thing, and I will never forgive this country for that.

That's all I'm going to say about it….

It's over.

One of the most important things Pam encouraged me to do was to let things go, and I've done just that, to a point.

After lunch, I go back out to the garage and tinker with the Mustang for the rest of the afternoon. I hear them talking about the fair on the radio. It starts tomorrow. The Western Washington State Fair grounds are about five blocks from my house. That means bad traffic for the next two weeks, but I don't care. I've lived here long enough to know my way around. I like the smells of the fair anyway, and I like the era of excitement the fair seems to generate.

They start to play music on the radio again, they kick off another guaranteed forty minutes of non-stop rock and roll with "Fooled Around and Fell in Love," by Alvin Bishop. I grab my half inch drive socket set, and I have no idea where the rest of the afternoon went to. I see Pam in a bikini swim suit walking the beach at Salt Water Park on a hot day, while I put a coat of wax on the El Camino in the shade of the fir trees that grew along the edge of the park.

I see the sway of her hips and I watch the wind tug on her long blonde hair. I loved her then, and I love her now, and I think about the ring in her jewelry box up in my bedroom. I'm ready to take it to her. I want to be with her. I want to touch her again. I want to hear her voice and see her smile.

I guess that's where my afternoon went. It went to memories of a better place and a better time.

I'm showered and shaved by six-thirty. I drive to the mall without much thought to anything, and I'm immediately angered when I find Becky at the fountain.

I see right away that Eric has slapped her around again.

She is bruised under one eye and she walks as though her ribs are hurting on her left side.

I don't screw around at the fountain. I make one lap and head off to my truck.

I have the engine fired and idling when she climbs in. I'm already moving as she closes her door.

"Matt," she says. "Don't. You know he did this because of last night. His friends came by with some meth as he was getting ready for work. I told him I am going to leave him."

"About time," I growl as I swing out of the mall parking lot and head for the freeway.

"He thinks I was with you last night. He thinks I'm going to move in with you."

I say nothing. I'm driving hard.

"I spent the night in my car, Matt. I was parked about a block from your house. I don't want to push myself on you, but just being close to you made me feel safer."

I glance at her.

She is crying.

I look away.

"I know you don't love me," she says.

I say nothing. I swing north bound on the I-5 and drive to Fife. I take an exit to the Tide Flats and head straight west toward Commencement Bay. I do not know what fabrication shop Eric works at, but I know his Tahoe. I will find him and kick the shit out of him just as I've promised him I would.

Becky cries for a few minutes, and then she tells me, "You know this is what he wants. He probably has his friends waiting for you. Please stop, Matt and think about this."

I drive on, we are now in the heart of the industrial area. The air smells of the bay and of plywood mills and iron works. The sky is a deep shade of grey and the rain is picking up. I turn on my wipers.

Becky says, "I'm sorry. This is all my fault. I've dragged you into my mess and I'm sorry. I should have left you alone."

I see a turn-out for trucks to check their loads and I pull into it. I park and leave the engine running. My wiper blades slide over the windshield intermittently. I look at Becky.

She is wearing blue jeans and a pink cotton sweater. She is wearing sandals. Her toe and finger nails are the same shade of pink as her sweater. Her hair is brushed out over her shoulders. She is sitting all the way over against her door with her hands in her lap. She smells of rain and a mild perfume. Her green eyes are wet and slightly red around the edges.

I shake my head, and look out the window toward the tide flats. I watch the rain fall into the sand and mud and tall weeds along the road. I think about the first time I slept with her. I wanted her as much as she wanted me.

"Not all your fault," I say. "You were confused, Becky. You were lonely and hurt and I just happened into your life. I was lonely and believe me, I wanted you. I could have said no. I didn't have to let you see the house. I didn't have to let you in. And no, I don't love you in a way that a man loves his wife or girlfriend, but I care about you a lot."

She smiles as she reaches over and touches my hand.

"I'm angry, but not at you," I say. "A reporter for the TNT came by today. She does a column, takes cold stories and revitalizes them. She's been snooping around. She must have talked with Duck, and sooner or later she will find you and maybe even Eric. I'm not ashamed of you, but I'm not proud of our relationship and it angers me to think people will find out about us."

Becky smiles. "Poor Matt. Sill living in the seventies. People won't think less of you for having slept with me. And you still stood up to Eric. You are still my hero."

I shake my head.

Becky leans across the seat and kisses my cheek.

"Do you need to see a doctor?" I ask.

She says, "No. He didn't pound on me real hard. I think he just wanted to draw you out. I really do."

"Wanna find out if that's true?" I ask.

Becky looks out the windshield at our surroundings. "I've been to his Fab shop before. I think you need to go right on the next street and it's up on the left. Back before he started doing meth, when we were madly in love, I used to bring his lunch to him, and we'd get worked up and do it in his Tahoe."

She giggles at the memory.

I sigh and put the truck in gear.

I drive up to the four-way stop and turn right. We travel down the road a short way, and then we see the large grey and blue building.

"That's it," says Becky. "The parking lot is up on the left, but there's a road before that I think goes around back."

I see the road she's talking about, and I turn left on it. It takes us along the back side of the parking lot. I drive down about half way and pull over.

All the vehicles in the lot are facing away from us. We are parked in a rear entrance where supply trucks probably go to unload heavy sheets of steel and angle iron around back. The road is slightly higher than the lot, but there are tall weeds growing close to the shoulder.

We see Eric's Tahoe right away. We figure his friends will park close to it.

Becky says, "Do you see the blue clunker five cars over from Eric's car? It's a Dodge something or other. A real piece of junk."

I climb out of my truck and stand on the running board. I'm high enough to see all of the lot now, and I pick up the dark blue Dodge Charger that has seen better days. And I see three silhouettes, moving around inside. I wonder if they are snorting more speed to stay on edge. I wonder if they have any weapons.

I climb back inside my cab and close the door. I put the truck in gear and do a K turn on the gravel road.

Becky and I are quiet until we are a couple of blocks away from the Dodge and its three occupants. I feel nervous and my palms are sweaty. I realize how close I came to getting my ass kicked. I have no second thoughts about that. They would have stamped my envelope. I would have never made it inside the building. No telling where they would have dumped me when they were finished working me over, but it would have been away from the fab shop. Maybe out on the tide flats, maybe up on north hill. And they would have done something to Becky to. She would have been a witness.

I feel old and foolish.

Becky says, "They are scary people, Matt. Eric thinks they are friends, but I think they are using him to buy crank because he has a job and he has money."

"Could be," I say. "In any case Eric shouldn't want them around you."

She scoots to the middle of the seat and puts a hand on my thigh. "I'm hungry, Matt. Can we eat now?"

I know she feels safe with me.

I wish she wouldn't.

Chapter Eleven

I drive us out to Lakewood and we eat at Deny's.

Becky's choice, not mine.

I have coffee and a piece of cheery pie. Becky devours a grand slam breakfast. I wonder how long it's been since she's had a meal. I feel sorry for her and I know that I cannot make her feel unwanted again. I don't want her sleeping in her car around the corner, but I can't have her sleeping in my bed either.

I don't know what to do with her.

Maybe I should put her up in a motel, this would be a short term arrangement, and it wouldn't cost me a lot of money. I would be helping her, and buying time to figure something out.

"How much money do you have?" I ask.

She chews on the last bite of a pancake as she shrugs. "Forty bucks maybe. Eric's good about giving me a little money every week. He wants me to buy food for his lunches. He makes good money. Sometimes I take a little of it while he's past out. He don't seem to notice." She pauses and a tear slides down her cheek. "Before he got hooked on meth, we had a pretty normal life. He was working the day shift, for a while, seven to four. An hour off for lunch. He's always made good money. We always had food and money left over to do things."

I nod. I want her to say more, but she goes quiet.

I prop my elbow up on the table and rest my chin against my fist. I gaze out the window for a moment and see wet cars on wet asphalt, and people hurrying in and out of the entrance.

Becky says, "Can I stay with you tonight?"

I choose my words carefully. "It's better if you don't, Becky. But I'll help you get a room at a motel not far from my place. We'll hide your car around back so no one will know you are there. You won't be far from me, and you can call and talk to me whenever you like."

She shrugs.

"It's only temporary until we can figure something out."

I know she doesn't like the idea, but I also know she is beginning to realize that we cannot be together. We cannot be lovers. And I truly feel that she will someday find a good young man to take care of her, and she'll realize how foolish it was for her to have had a relationship with me.

After dinner, I drive us back to the mall for Becky's car. I follow her out to Puyallup where we swing by the house she and Eric live in. Becky runs inside to pack a small bag. I climb out of my truck and wait on the front porch.

This house is about eight blocks from mine. It was probably built in the late fifties or early sixties. It is one story with a low pitch on the roof, and it has a car port instead of a garage. The yard is un-kept, weeds growing everywhere, and an ugly chain link fence follows the property line.

I think about the eight blocks to my house. There has to be a few corner stores in that distance, and Becky picks the closest one. I can think of a few reasons why, and a few reasons why not, but it doesn't really matter anymore.

Becky is inside for maybe thirty minutes. She comes out swinging a small green suitcase and her giant leather purse.

She follows me into downtown, and we drive south on Meridian to the College Court Motel.

I pay in cash for two nights. I go inside with her and check the room out. It is small, but clean and comfortable. It is about five minutes from my house if you drive the speed limit. It comes with cable TV, free coffee and doughnuts. We'd stopped at a quick stop up the street and Becky bought a bottle of Boone's Farm wine.

I ask for her cell phone number.

She rights it down on a piece of hotel stationary and hands it to me.

We are quiet for a few moments.

She is sitting on the edge of the bed, and I'm standing at the door with my hand on the knob.

"Okay?" I ask

"Guess so," she sighs.

"It's only temporary."

She nods as she stares down at her hands in her lap.

I want to take her in my arms and comfort her.

I want to be young enough to be her man.

But I can't and I'm not, and I leave out of there feeling rough about the whole thing. I think about the eight blocks and all the stores, and I decide that is was simply meant to happen.

But that didn't make it right.

It is nine-thirty when I enter my home.

The phone is ringing and I pick it up in the living room.

"Hello, Matt," says Faye.

"Hi."

"Am I bothering you?"

"Nope."

"Can we talk a while?"

"Sure."

She sighs, and then she says, "There was a reporter here today. Some woman with the TNT. She asked me a bunch of questions about you."

"She was here too," I say.

"I thought some of her questions were a little odd. She seemed to be snooping for dirt on you. I straightened her out, told her what a dear and precious hero you really are."

"Thanks, Faye," I rasp as I wonder if now's the time to tell her about Becky.

She sighs, and then starts in on a long story about her second husband who owned a string of warehouses. She didn't really love him, but he was nice to her and he had inherited a lot of money when his mother past away, so they lived very comfortably in a mansion that stood on a golf course out in Redman. He loved to play golf, of course, and he died on the fourteenth hole from a massive heart attack one day.

I notice that in all of Faye's stories about her husbands, they have money, they are nice to her, and she is true to them. And I believe that in her own way, Faye is trying to tell me about herself as much as she is the people of her life.

She tells me goodnight around ten-fifteen, and I smile as I hang up the phone.

I think about Becky for a moment. I rise from my recliner and go out onto the back porch. I lift the flower pot and pick up the key. I carry it inside and put it on the pegboard. I lock the back door, and check the front door. I turn on the porch light and retrieve my .357 from the coat closet in the hallway.

I return to my recliner and switch on the TV.

As I watch some late news, I call Becky's cell.

She sounds a little drunk when she answers the phone.

"You okay?"

"Up."

"Has Eric called you?"

"Up."

"What did you tell him, Becky?"

"Nothing. He said he gets home I better be there. I hung up on em."

"Ok. Why don't you turn your phone off so he can't keep calling and bothering you. You might say something to give away your location. You can call me anytime you need to, but you don't need to be talking to him right now."

"Okay," she says, "I'll put it in airplane mode."

"Whatever that is," I say. "Just make sure he can't bother you."

She sighs into the phone.

"This is only temporary, Becky. I promise. Please try to get some sleep. He won't find you unless you tell him where you're at."

She sighs again, and hangs up.

I'm waiting for them when they arrive. I'm at the window with the gun, and I've left the porch light on in hopes of getting a better glimpse of Eric's three companions. I like to know my enemies. If they know me, but I don't know them, they have an advantage. I need to have some idea of their sizes and facial appearances.

It could come in handy.

They are driving the clunker tonight.

They creep up to my house real slow, and stop just inside the patch of white light coming from my front porch. They know I'm watching, and they smile. They know I want to see them, and they give me a good look.

All three of them are skinny, most meth freaks are. All three of them probably have bad teeth and smell of body odor. The driver has a pale complexion. The two in the back seat are darker, maybe Hispanic, maybe not. The driver has light brown hair and he is talking to Eric as he grins up at my window.

Eric nods and says something to the one behind him in the back seat, who climbs out of the car and walks around to the small gate in my white picket fence. He gives me a very good look of his face, and I see that he is not Hispanic, just dark, and he is the largest of the four. He is wearing a muscle shirt and his arms are covered with tattoos. His eyes are coal black. He has a pistol tucked into his belt. He turns to make sure I see it. He chuckles, unzips his pants and relieves himself on my fence. All the while, he is staring up at me.

He takes his time, shakes it defiantly, flips me off and then walks around and climbs back into the car.

Eric nods his head at me as they slowly pull away from the curb.

I sleep in the recliner again, with the loaded gun this time, and for the life of me, I do not feel as scared as I think I should be.

I learned to sleep in my clothes and how to deal with fear in Vietnam.

In the jungles of Binh Duong province there was a secret zone where it was believed the Chinese trained terrorists. They sent them to Saigon to kill Americans. They supplied them with guns, bombs and money.

We never found the secret zone, but our scouts found several trails they believed were being used as supply routes.

We set up ambushes along the trails.

The jungle cools off at night and becomes a silent sheet of darkness. I remember the silence. I remember the darkness.

Believe me, you may think you know them, but you don't know shit.

I remember sleeping in my clothes with a loaded rifle. I remember waking to the sound of someone moving on the trail. I remember my heart hitting like a Ball Peen hammer in my chest. I remember the air in my lungs feeling too thick to breathe.

Adrenaline.

I'm amazed at what thrill seekers do to feel the rush. Bungee jumping, skydiving, and somersaults on a motorcycle--the list goes on.

I could save them a lot of money if I could give them my nightmares.

Chapter Twelve

Saturday morning is clear and cold. A light layer of frost covers the ground. The sky is pale blue with clouds like smears of white paint along the edges of it, and the river carries down the chill of fall from the Cascade Mountains where there is snow on the high peaks.

It is the first weekend of the State Fair. By noon the air is filled with the sounds and smells of animals, greasy food, people and traffic. Pam and I used to get excited about the fair. We'd go at least twice. Once to see the exhibits and once to see a rock and roll show.

I think I'll pass on it this year.

Sometimes the weather cooperates with the fair, and sometimes it doesn't. This year it starts out looking pretty good. By two in the afternoon, it is nearly eighty degrees out.

Dick and Silva have me over around four.

I'd been up since eight. Dick had called at nine to remind me of the invitation. I'd tinkered with the Mustang for a while, and I'd pulled some weeds from the flower beds along the back porch. I thought of reasons not to go, but none were good enough to use.

Faye called at noon to invite me over for lunch.

I told her I was eating an early dinner at Dick and Silva's.

She didn't seem too happy about that. "Well okay then," she said. "If that's what you want to do."

"I'm not thrilled," I said. "But they have been friends for a long time, and we don't get together very often anymore. I feel I should do this."

She told me she understood and hung up.

I don't know what to think of that.

I'd called Becky at two and she seemed to be doing okay. She sounded a little hung over. She told me she was going to run up to the mall later and find a book to read.

I told her I was going to be busy tonight, but that I'd come by early on Sunday morning, and we'd figure something out.

She seemed fine with that.

So I wasn't worried about her when I went next door.

I'm fresh from a long shower. I'm shaved and wearing clean blue jeans and a button down cotton shirt and my new shoes.

A large charcoal grill is standing in the center of Dick's patio. He is smiling, sipping on a tall Vodka Collins, and flipping rib eyes. He has a radio playing country music from its perch on the sundeck railing.

Silva meets me at the front door with a cold beer. She gives me a peck on the cheek and asks how I'm doing.

"Okay," I tell her.

She points at Dick through the window. "He's on his second drink, one of us better check the steaks."

I laugh, and she heads off into her kitchen.

I go out through the French doors onto the sundeck and step down to the patio.

There are four chairs set up at a small table. I plop down in one of the chairs and Dick says, "If I remember right, you like them well done."

"Yup."

He closes the lid on his grill and brings his drink to the table. He sits down and sighs, "We're sort of dragging our feet. There's one more guest."

"Oh yea."

Silva comes out with dishes and silverware. "How we doing?"

Dick rolls his eyes as he gets up to check on the steaks.

I watch Silva set the table for four. I'm about to ask her about the fourth guest, but she rushes back off into the house.

Dick hums along with a song by Lady Antebellum.

I gaze off at the little kids playing in the back yard opposite of mine to Dick and Silva's. I wonder how things would have been for Pam and me if she'd been able to have them. She loved kids. She wanted kids. We would have never bought the old house. It would have been to much work with kids around, and Pam would have never been lonely while I was away on the rigs in Alaska.

Dick calls out, "Steaks ready, Silva dear."

I decide to use the restroom now. That way I won't have to get up during the meal.

"Be right back," I say.

He nods and smiles. Dick sort of looks like a football player with a beer belly. He has the shoulders and arms, but the tummy don't fit. He is handsome and always cheerful.

His eyes are light brown and his hair is black with streaks of grey running through it. We've never had enough in common to be friends, but we've always liked and trusted each other.

I stand and move across the patio. I climb the steps onto the sundeck and angle toward the French doors. Once inside the house I turn down the hallway toward the restroom, but I make it only half way to the door.

"Matt," calls Silva. "Hang on a second." She rushes from the kitchen area carrying a bowl of potato salad.

I stop and turn to her.

Silva is pretty. She has auburn hair and bright hazel eyes. She is small and athletic. She is very smart, and she was a good friend to Pam. She used to let Pam watch her kids when they were little. She knew how much that meant to Pam, and actually asked her to watch the kids sometimes even when she didn't need a sitter.

I smile.

She moves in close to me. "I'm not trying to start any trouble," she says. "I know you and Faye are seeing each other, but I really feel you should play the field a little before you get settled again."

"Don't worry about that," I sigh.

"I know you must get very lonely," she says. "Faye can be pushy. She's a dear person, but…."

"I know," I say.

"You are handsome. You need to remember that. There are a lot of women I know who would love to meet you."

"And?"

Her eyes sparkle. "I promised Pam I would look after you."

I nod.

"So," she says. "You want to meet one of my friends?"

"I don't know," I say.

"Oh come on. I've shown your picture to her and she is dying to meet you."

"You have a picture of me?"

"On my cell phone. It was taken right out back last summer."

I shake my head at her.

She scowls. "Faye is a trophy hunter, Matt. You don't know her like I do. She'll win you over and parade you around in front of her rich friends, and then tire of you and dump you."

I think about that. I don't see it the way Silva does, but I'm not sure about myself, or Faye, at the moment.

Silva says, "Believe me, Faye is a gold digger, but she isn't always after money. Sometimes the prize is worth more."

I shrug.

"Just tell me you'll be careful."

"Okay," I say. "I'll be careful."

"And you'll meet one of my friends?"

"Okay."

She does a victory pump with one arm and swings away.

I watch her go, and I realize the true reason for this dinner was just presented to me. I shake my head.

Autumn is seated in the fourth chair on the patio when I return from the restroom. She is large, not fat, maybe what Becky will look like if she takes care of herself when she reaches her fifties. Autumn has hair the color of ginger and she wears it in a stream of curls that flow down to her shoulders. Her eyes are blue. She is wearing white shorts and a red blouse. Her finger and toe nails are the same color red as her lips. She smiles and rises as I approach the table. She is pretty. I like her nose and her chin.

"Sorry to be late," she says. "Got held up in the fair traffic."

"Autumn Cane, this is Matt Conner," says Silva.

We shake hands and allow our eyes to hold briefly.

I'm home by seven.

It was a good dinner. I'm stuffed, I've had three beers, and I have Autumn's phone number.

I plop down in my big easy chair and use the remote to turn on the TV and find a good college football game. By finding a good one I mean finding one that is not lopsided. College football can go one of three ways, good, bad, and ugly. On any given Saturday you can take your pick. I find a good one and settle in and think about Autumn.

She's attractive. She gave me the feeling she's available, but not desperate. I like that, and I like the way she asked for my phone number in return for hers, and the way she touched my arm when I walked her to her 1978 red and white refurbished Corvette. She told me she was a sucker for old cars.

I like the touch of hardness around her eyes, and in the set of her chin. I like that we don't have much in common, except old cars and loneliness. She left me feeling a little excited about seeing her again, maybe, I don't know.

I smile and stop thinking about her, and start to follow the game.

Faye calls during half time.

We talk about the fair traffic jamming up town for a few moments, and then she tells me about her third husband, the only one she came close to loving. He was the vice president of a West Coast food store chain. He loved race horses and spent a lot of his free time at the tracks. He used to take Faye with him. They took the company Leer and flew to wherever there was a race. He never bet on the horses. He only invested in them, and he loved to watch them run.

He died of a rare blood disease. He was nearly seventy. He never saw it coming. He'd always felt healthy and saw no reason for checkups. One day he woke up sick and stayed sick until he died. He was the one who'd left Faye the most, and she was still getting his share of stud fees from some of the horses he'd invested in.

Faye ends her story, and she's quiet a moment, and then she says, "By the way, I have to run out to Bremerton tomorrow. I have an aunt in a home out there that I haven't visited in a while. Would you like to tag along, we'll make a day out of it."

I'm thinking this would be date number three, but I'm also thinking that I have to check on Becky. Reluctantly I say, "I have a few errands to run myself tomorrow."

She hesitates. "I hope they don't include the redhead with that old car."

I sigh and scratch my forehead as I rasp, "Autumn's a friend of Silva's from work."

"Oh, well, none of my business anyway, Matt. Sorry I brought it up."

"Faye…" I start and stop.

"Yes, Matt."

"Nothing."

She blurts, "Did Silva say anything about me?"

"No. It was just a dinner and her friend was there, that's all."

She's hesitates and then she says, "Well. I'll talk to you tomorrow evening, if that's okay."

"Sure," I say.

After we hang up, I think about Silva's take on Faye. If Silva is correct, should I care? I don't believe so. Faye is fun to be with. I'm not lonesome when I'm with her, but I do not love her, and she is not going to break my heart no matter what her intentions are.

I remember how Pam didn't care much for football, but she always snuggled in the chair with me during a game. Sometimes she'd take a sip of my beer. At half time, I'd get up to pee, and Pam would fetch some snacks from the kitchen.

She was a good wife.

I'll never find another one like her.

I suddenly find myself crying silent tears and wanting another beer.

I was once a very heavy drinker. Whiskey was my anodyne.

I feel I'm backsliding now. It takes more and more beer to fill the void in my life and put me to sleep. I feel weak and sinful. I feel as though I'm falling down.

I have no one to blame.

No one has twisted my arm.

It's always been my choice.

I like it quiet and I like to be alone, but I'm beginning to realize these things are not good for me.

I need someone to talk to. Someone who understands me. I need more than sex. I need a companion.

With Becky it's all about sex, and it's as much my fault as hers.

I feel I've betrayed Pam with that relationship.

I need Pam.

People don't know me. She did. She knew what I was capable of doing.

She helped me live through the nightmares and cold sweat. She was there for me when I woke from a nap on the couch and wasn't sure of where I was at.

She helped me deal with the guilt and the anger.

She helped me put the whiskey bottle down.

She loved me.

I miss her and want to join her. I want to take the ring to her.

Sometimes I feel I should go upstairs and run the tub full of cold water. I'll take the ring, a bottle of whiskey and a loaded gun. I'll climb into the tub and go find her.

I never dreamed I would be this lonesome without her. I used to work a two weeks on and two weeks off schedule in Alaska, but I was able to call Pam every day after work. Sometimes I'd call her before work. Just knowing she was waiting for me. Just knowing she missed me as much as I missed her was always enough to get me through.

And we had one way of doing things on the day I'd come home. We'd make love and then I'd unpack my bags.

It never felt dirty with Pam.

It never felt wrong.

The telephone wakes me. The TV is still on, but the game has finished hours ago. It is late. I think it is Becky calling.

"Low," I say.

Eric says, "What are you doing old man?"

My throat goes dry. My heart hits like a hammer.

He chuckles, "Where is she, asshole?"

I gain some composure. "What do you want?"

"Want my girl, fuck-head."

"Makes you think I know where she is."

"Oh you know, old man. You probably got her with you. I might just come on in and find out."

My head swings to the front door. I think about my .357 in the closet.

I tell Eric, "Don't make this personal."

"Personal, shit. I'll fuck you up old man."

"You've been warned," I say.

He laughs and hangs up.

I crawl from the chair and walk to the front door. I gaze out through the little window on top.

The Tahoe is parked at the curb. The porch light is off. All I can see are shadows, and I see four of them moving around inside the Tahoe. They drive off slowly.

I'm shaking when I dial Becky's number.

She answers on the fifth ring. She sounds sleepy.

"Sorry," I say. Just checking on you."

"Okay, Matt."

"See you in the morning."

"Kay."

My emotions are all tangled up when I go to bed. I'm angry and scared. I feel foolish, and reckless, and yet I feel in control of it all.

I have the gun with me.

I open Pam's jewelry box and while it jingles the Carol King song, "You've got a friend," I stare at the ring.

For the life of me I don't know why, but I think about Whiskey.

Chapter Thirteen

B ecky tells me she is not going to spend another night in this dump. "Or any other dump in town," she adds.

She is sitting in a chair by the window. She has her bag packed. She is wearing white jeans and a yellow blouse. She has fixed her hair. She is wearing makeup. She looks cute, and she is pouting.

It is nine in the morning.

I should be at home getting ready for the first NFL football game.

I watch the play of teal light in her eyes for a moment, and then I tell her about Eric's phone call.

She shakes her head.

"I don't want you staying in a motel either," I say. "But I can't have you staying with me."

"Then I'll go home. Maybe Eric has learned his lesson."

"There has to be someone else in your life, Becky. Someone you can turn to."

"No," she cries. "No one."

I pace the floor. I feel the situation with her is hopeless, and I am out of ideas. I want to go home and forget about the whole thing, and I'm beginning to feel it's the only option I have left. If she gets hurt, so be it. Her problem is not mine anymore.

Her cell phone suddenly vibrates. She looks at it. "Eric," she says, "I'm going to talk to him."

I turn and leave. I walk out to my truck and climb in. I fire up the engine and let it idle. I gaze out at the clear morning sky. The air smells of the river and turning leaves and the fair.

I wait fifteen minutes.

Becky comes out swinging her purse and the small suitcase. She sees me and angles over to my truck. "I'm going home," she says.

I nod.

She smiles at me for a moment, and then she walks to her car. I watch the way her hips sway in the tight jeans. I notice her panty lines. I watch her climb into the Toyota and drive away.

I don't feel good about it, but I let it go.

I have to.

I'm home in time for kick-off.

I feel as though I have my life back. I've made a clear decision. Becky is an adult. She can take care of herself.

I worry a little about her, but by noon I'm on my first beer and thinking about Pam.

I'm thinking about the time we drove the coast all the way from Seattle to Southern California. It was right after I'd retired and a few months before she became sick.

We had the rest of our lives to grow old together.

We had enough money to do so in reasonable comfort.

We still loved each other as much or more as we did the day we were married.

This was our retirement celebration trip. It was late summer. The weather was beautiful. We stopped and enjoyed the sunset every night.

We acted like a couple of kids. Why not? We had no worries.

Pam had bought sexy things to wear to bed at night. She made every moment seem special, and when I think back on it now, I can't help but wonder if she didn't already know she was sick, but she didn't want to tell me.

I remember she insisted I get a physical every year. She told me I was at that age where it was important. Especially the blood work. They can find things early through your blood.

Was she making sure I wasn't infected?

I drink beer and watch football all afternoon. I watch the highlights and eat a sandwich before the Sunday night game. I take a nap in my chair, but I wake up in time to catch most of the second half, which is well worth seeing because the Lions come back and beat the Eagles by three.

I turn off the TV.

The phone rings.

I decide not to answer it because it might be Becky and I don't want to hear it anymore. I want it to be over with. I want to move on with my miserable life.

The key is still out back. I figure if she's in trouble, she'll come over anyway, and this time I'll tell her she has to leave, because I am finished helping her.

At mid-night I'm standing on my front porch with a loaded .357. I'm thinking when Eric shows up I'm going to fire a round over his head and tell him it's over.

Lucky for him and me, he doesn't drive by tonight.

I don't remember what time I go to bed. I think I'm a little drunk, and that's what helps me sleep so hard.

No anxiety, no bad thoughts on my conscience. Just black, blank sleep.

Chapter Fourteen

M onday, Faye calls at ten.

I'm not doing anything. I'm sitting in front of the television, but it is not on. I had turned if off a couple hours ago, after I'd heard the news. I have a headache, and I my mouth is as dry as the state of Arizona.

I need to do laundry and pay bills today.

I need to vacuum the rugs.

Faye asks, "Did you have a good Sunday?"

I can tell by the sound of her voice she's still a little hurt that I didn't go to Bremerton with her.

I say, "I took care of my errands and was home in time to watch football and drink beer all day and half the night."

She is quiet while she absorbs that.

"How is your aunt?" I ask.

She says, "I wonder why I bother seeing her sometimes. It takes nearly an hour before she realizes who I am."

I nod and wait.

"I tried to call you when I got home," she says. "Your truck was parked out front, but you didn't answer your phone."

I remember the phone ringing, and thinking it might be Becky.

"I must have fallen asleep. Sometimes a boring game will do that."

Faye says, "You shouldn't be home alone so much, Matt. It's not good for you. I'm not trying to be pushy. I worry about you."

"I know, and I appreciate it."

"Did Silva say anything about us Saturday when you were over there for dinner?"

"Not really."

She is quiet again.

"Why would she?" I ask.

"Silva and I are not on the best of terms. Probably why she had a friend over for you to meet."

I think about that for a moment, and I decide to tell her part of the truth. "Silva promised Pam she'd look out for me. She is worried I spend a lot of time home alone, so she asked me to meet one of her friends. Silva is aware of you and I seeing each other, she did mention it, but it was no big deal."

"Did you like her friend?"

"She was okay."

"That's an evasive answer."

"We hardly talked. We ate. I don't really know her."

"You walked her to her car. You exchanged phone numbers."

I'm quiet as I wonder why Faye wants to pick a fight over this. It was really nothing in my book.

She says, "You must have found something about her that you liked."

"Her Corvette," I reply.

"Huh. That old car."

"How about a date tonight?" I blurt. "I'll take you out and tell you all about my lunch at Dick and Silva's."

"No thanks," she says and hangs up.

I smile and shake my head.

I figure she wants to think about what I've said, and I think she wants me to maybe chase her a little. That would prove something to her, I guess. I don't remember a fight in the three date ritual. Maybe Faye just tacked one on there.

Thanks to Bayer Aspirin, by noon I'm all cleaned up and ready to start my day. I check the mail and pay the bills first, and then I take my truck into town and wash her up at a wand-wash place that still only charges a dollar to get the pump started.

I wipe the old girl down with soft cloths, and I vacuum out the inside. I use some Armor-all wipes on the dash and Windex on the windows. After that, I drive over to Duck's store for some beer.

I set a half rack of Ice House down on the sales counter and Duck rings it up.

"How is life?" he asks.

"It's good," I say.

"Lady from newspaper come by and ask many questions." I nod.

"I mind own business," he says. "I say very little to her." I smile.

He gives me my change.

"Thanks, Duck."

He nods his head. He doesn't know that the very little he said to her was enough for her to draw conclusions and make subtle accusations. I'd thought about buying a Sunday paper just to see what she had to say, but I didn't really care.

Why should I?

I tinker with the Mustang until four in the afternoon, and then I decide to call Faye. Why? I'm not sure, but I think it's because I'm attracted to her, and that I have been for a long time. I also think she's got her hook set in me. After all, didn't she chase me first?

She answers after several rings.

"How about dinner and a movie?" I ask.

"No thank you," she says.

"Okay." I start to hang up, but she shouts my name.

"Matt are you there? Can you hear me?"

"Yes."

"Were you about to hang up?

"Yup."

She's quiet.

I wait her out.

"I'll have dinner ready at six," she says and hangs up.

I realize I'm going to miss Monday Night Football, and I'm wondering if Faye is worth it.

I'm guessing she is. Monday Night Football isn't half the show it used to be anyway. I miss Howard and Don and Frank. I miss the reverse angle re-play. I miss the way a game used to be covered. I miss the original theme song, and I miss Hank Williams Junior.

Monday Night Football says a lot about the way things used to be in America. We used to be entitled to our opinion. Remember?

I take a shower and shave. I splash on some Usher.

I'm wearing a pair of slacks and a button down shirt when I go next door. I'm feeling good about this.

I think Pam is smiling.

I know she wouldn't want me to sit at home and drink another night away.

Chapter Fifteen

Faye can cook. I figure she can probably make old boot leather taste good.

She's wearing a nice outfit. A black and red evening gown that slides along the curves of her body and shows one heck of a lot of cleavage.

We eat by candle light and make small talk about the neighborhood and how it has changed in the last few years. We stay away from the subject of Silva and the dinner Saturday afternoon.

The wine is red and I can't pronounce the name of it.

Faye has a sparkle in her eyes, and her perfume captivates me.

When we are finished eating, she clears the table and loads the dish washer. I wonder if I should thank her and leave.

She returns to the table, sits down and sips her wine, and then she folds her hands in her lap and stares into the space between us.

I'm not sure about what I should say or do. I know I want her tonight, but I'm not sure if she wants me. What if she wants to wait a little longer? Maybe three dates and a little fight is not enough. Maybe she's decided I'm just another good listener and eater.

Hell, I don't know.

So I dive right in. "That was a good meal, thank you."

"You're welcome."

"Should I leave?"

"No."

"I've never been real good at this other part," I say.

She lifts her eyes to mine and asks in a deep timbre, "Do I have to beg you?"

I smile and stand up. I help her from her chair and we start to kiss. She tastes better than I'd thought she would.

Before I know it, she is the only thing in the world that I am aware of. We kiss and feel of each other all the way into her bedroom where it is pretty and smells nice.

She blushes as she undresses slowly in front of me. She is wearing a red one piece silk thing. She turns the zipper in back to me. I oblige, and I can't help but notice her firm soft white curves. She moves to the bed before she lets the red silk fall. She climbs under the covers and tucks an arm behind her head.

I pull my clothes off with reckless abandon.

Faye laughs.

The moment we join under the covers, I know it's right, but I feel guilty and I know in my heart that I should have told her about Becky. I should have let her know what I did, and see if she still feels the same way about me.

But I also feel this isn't the time to bring it up.

I wake at five.

I feel that something is wrong.

I gently lift Faye's hand from my hairy chest, and crawl out of her bed. I have a slight headache, and my mouth is dry. I dress quietly and carry my new shoes down the stairs to the front porch.

I lock her door as I leave.

The morning is cold and clear.

I wave at the paper carrier as I cross Faye's yard and step onto mine. Something catches my eye right away, and I stop. I back up a little and look at my truck parked in its little spot out at the curb.

"Dirty old cradle robber," is painted across the tailgate in bold red letters.

I move in for a closer look and notice that the paint is permanent.

Chapter Sixteen

I remove the tailgate from my truck and hide it in the detached garage. I feel the angry spirit waking up inside me as I walk to the back porch and check under the flower pot for the spare key.

It is there.

Something is out of kilter.

I stare at the phone while the coffee brews. I expect it to ring, but it doesn't.

I have a cell phone, but I haven't used it since Pam died. She had insisted I carry one whenever I was away from her. No need carrying it now, but for some reason I felt compelled to find it and charge it up. It is in the top drawer of Pam's computer desk. I take it out and plug it in. I've been paying the phone bill every month. I think it still works.

I turn on the TV and sip my first cup of coffee. They are talking about the scandals in Washington DC. I can't help but remember a book that was published when Bush was president. The title of the book was "Dude Where's my Country?" Or something like that. I can't help but wonder if the author had found his country now, and if this is what he actually had in mind.

I have to shake my head at it all.

I miss Nixon. At least he tried to win the war in Vietnam. It's just that the congress was overrun with chicken-shits at the time, and they wouldn't let him level Hanoi. That's why he pulled the plug on the whole thing.

Nixon was a mess, I'll agree with that, but he wasn't so bad when you compare him to the people who've been in Washington the last few years.

Troubling things come to mind. Things that are not good for our country. It's hard to believe that anyone who lives in America and enjoys her freedom would want to destroy her. Yet sometimes that seems to be the case, and it's not just the president. He has lots of help because restructuring America is a big job.

We all learned a lesson from 9-11, but the gist of what happened is fading away. I hope and pray nothing like that ever happens again, but it sure seems to me we are on the wrong road to avoiding it. I don't have a college degree, but I think kissing our enemy's ass is not working. There's a lot of other things not working too, free things, that have nothing to do with freedom, and everything to do with entitlement.

My wife, Pam was pretty liberal when I married her, and I was extremely conservative. As time went on, we rubbed off on each other. We were registered as independent voters, but we leaned to the conservative side of most major issues. Especially abortion.

Pam was one of countless women in the world who couldn't have children. It was obvious where she stood on the issue, and she could get pretty worked up over it at times. She called it murder, clear and simple.

I think about it now, and wish we'd have adopted a couple kids for her. I know we came close to checking into it a few times, but I still can't recall the reasons we never got around to it.

I rub my tearful eyes and turn off the television.

Enough of that.

In the quiet, I feel restless. I stop thinking about Pam and start thinking about Becky. I'm worried, and I don't know why.

I remember the day I became her hero.

—ɷ—

It was two days after I'd met her. It was hot. Washington State is like that sometimes. In two days it can go from sixty to ninety and skip what's in between. I had mowed my yard and used the weed eater to trim around the edges of the flower beds.

Faye was in her garden, pulling weeds and trimming bushes. She had called to me over the fence, and I'd pretended not to hear her.

After I'd put the mower and Weed Eater away, I went inside for a cold beer. It was only two in the afternoon, and except on Sundays and Wednesdays, I normally try not to drink before four, but I was going to make an exception that day because of the heat.

There was no beer in the fridge. Had I drank an entire twelve pack in two days?

No. I'm not that bad yet.

I'd removed some of them and put them in the pantry to make room for food in the fridge. I could stuff a couple in the freezer and wait about thirty minutes, or head on over to Duck's store and buy some cold ones.

Not a tough decision for me.

I looked around for my truck keys, and found them, but I decided to walk anyway. Why not? It was a beautiful day. I was wearing a white muscle shirt and blue jeans. I had my wallet and house keys.

I was good to go.

I headed out, and I was thinking about what I might do next to the Mustang as I went along the sidewalk. Maybe I'd remove the intake manifold again just for the hell of it. Why not? No, I think I'd rather mess with the tranny some more, or maybe the rear end.

Five minutes later I was still tossing projects around in my head when I reached the store.

Duck waved at me as I entered, and I tossed him a grin as I turned for the beer cooler. Duck had a swinging pedestal fan running, and it tossed my hair around as I moved past the aisles. I swung left at the last one, and Becky was standing in front of the beer section.

She was wearing a pair of blue jean shorts that fit her tight, a yellow T-shirt and sandals. Her toe and finger nails were painted the same shade of pink as her lipstick. She was holding a bottle of Boons Farm wine and a six pack of Ice House.

She smiled and said, "Was on my way to see you. Thought you might like some company."

I was surprised, and it took me a few moments to recover. "That's not a good idea, Becky," I rasped slowly.

She turned her face and looked at me out the corners of her eyes. "You sure about that?"

I saw the slivers of teal.

"Yea. Pretty sure."

She shook her head.

I tried to move around her, but she grabbed my arm.

"Didn't it mean anything to you?"

I glanced down at my feet. "Of course it did. But that don't make it right."

She said, "Second time is supposed to be better."

"I know and maybe that's what scares me."

She giggled.

"Where's your man?"

"I don't know. Should be sleeping, but he's not."

I shrugged.

She said, "I know you're not seeing anyone right now."

I glanced away, and wondered how she could know that.

"Thought we hit if off pretty good the other day," she added.

"You don't want an old man like me," I sighed.

"You're not that old."

"I'm old enough to know this isn't right, Becky, and I don't think we should see each other again."

"Why not," she asked.

"Cause I don't want to."

"Matt..." she started.

I shook my head.

She moved her lips to say more, but let it go.

I took the six pack from her, turned and carried it to the sales counter.

Just as I set it down and dug out my wallet, Becky's man came walking in.

He was dark and tall and slender and all sweaty. He wore his hat backward. He tossed Duck and me a hard look as he stomped toward the beer coolers.

I suddenly felt as though my lungs were filled with heavy air.

Duck followed Eric with his eyes.

Three seconds of life vanished, and then....

"There you are, you drunken slut," he shouted.

"Eric," she called. "What are you doing? You should be sleeping."

"Shut up, bitch."

Duck and I heard what sounded like a ball bat striking wet sand, followed by the sound of heavy glass hitting the floor and shattering.

Duck reached for his telephone while I raced down the aisles of dry goods and canned food. The angry spirit was snapping inside me like a whip in dry air.

Eric had pinned Becky up against the cooler. He'd hit her in the stomach, and the face. He was reared back to hit her again when I reached them. I caught his arm and swung him around. I punched him three times in the face, jabs, nothing powerful enough to knock him out, but hard enough to do some damage.

He reeled back a little, stunned and covering up.

I pulled Becky from the cooler and shoved her behind me.

Eric squared off, but stopped.

He was bleeding from his nose and mouth, and one of his eyes was sort of puffy.

He glared at me, and then something clicked in the darkness behind his pupils.

"You know each other?" he growled.

"Yes," said Becky. She wrapped her arms around my stomach and pressed herself into my back.

Two seconds later, I watched the last tumbler fall into place in the one eye of his that wasn't swollen.

The way Becky was clinging to me and peering at him from around one of my shoulders didn't take a college degree to figure a connection.

He laughed and said, "You seeing this old man?"

"Yes," she spat at him.

"Police coming," called Duck from the sales counter.

Eric said, "You got to be shitting me."

Becky shook her head.

His face turned red as he doubled up his fists and began to move straight at me.

"You don't need more trouble with the cops," shouted Becky.

"They come, they come," called Duck.

Eric stopped. He wanted a big piece of me in a bad way, but his trouble with the law must have been pretty serious.

I took advantage of the moment.

"You think you're tough beating on a girl?" I snarled.

"Fuck you," he growled as he tried to gather himself, but I could see in his eyes that he wasn't sure about this.

I gained momentum.

"Don't touch her again," I said. "If you do, I will knock the shit out of you. You got that? You touch her and I'll break your fucking neck."

He tossed me an evil grin, turned and ran out of the store. He jumped into his Tahoe and broke the tires loose as he raced away.

I didn't need attention, and I wanted to get out of there before the police arrived, but Becky was hurt and I couldn't leave her.

There must have been a cruiser close by to take the call. Two officers were in the store and asking questions before I had helped Becky to the sales counter.

An ambulance was dispatched, and while we waited, Becky was interrogated by the police. In her signed statement she denied knowing her assailant, but her description of him was close to Duck's and mine. According to her, she was buying wine when she was suddenly assaulted. She believed her attacker was after her money. She was truly grateful that I had stepped in to stop him.

As they were loading her into the ambulance, she tossed me a curious look.

I gave her a blank stare.

The press picked up on her story and it escalated from there.

Becky never mentioned knowing me before hand, and Duck concentrated his story on the rescue. He told everyone how brave I was to save the girl from the hands of her assailant. How I charged in and stopped what could have been a robbery or rape. So the story went down as me being a hero by standing up to a neighborhood punk.

Thinking back on it now, I realize that Becky started the lie because she still loved Eric and didn't want him in trouble. I went along with it because I'm embarrassed of my affair with Becky and I didn't want it exposed. And Duck went along with it because in his own words, "I mind own business."

The amazing part was how fast they scrambled a film crew to Duck's store. In less than an hour, Duck and I were being interviewed on film.

It aired on the local news at ten that evening.

They cut five minutes of interview down to two, and most of it was Duck telling the story in an animated way that seemed almost comical, yet dramatic. The shots of me were brief, but important. The quiet hero, standing there, looking pudgy in the spot light, and letting Duck praise him for his heroic actions.

I should have told the truth immediately.

I had several chances and past on them. I should have told the police it was Eric Dawson, Becky's boyfriend. He beats on her all the time. He's a druggie. He drives a dark blue, late model Tahoe. No, I didn't get the plate number, but I'm sure Becky knows where he's at. They live together.

If I had told the truth, things would be different right now.

Chapter Seventeen

Faye calls at nine.

"You enjoy last night?"

"I did," I say.

"I did too," she says. "I'd like to do it again soon."

"Which part?" I ask.

I think she blushes. "All of it," she replies after a moment.

I think about the way she moaned and kissed my neck. I fall silent, lost for words.

Faye says, "But I have an important question for you."

"Okay."

"Last night when you called and asked me out, and I said no at first, were you going to call the red head next?"

"Autumn?"

"I believe that's her name, yes."

"I don't really know her, why would I."

"Your okay was pretty quick."

"Like maybe I had a backup plan."

"Yes, that's it."

I shake my head.

She says, "Well, am I right?"

"I hadn't thought of it, no. Guess I didn't have a backup plan."

She absorbs that and says, "Matt, for some reason I believe you."

"We good for tonight then?"

She chuckles. "No. My friends are coming over tonight. But I'm free tomorrow night."

"Sounds good," I say, and we hang up.

I drink more coffee and stare at the TV. I know something is terribly wrong in my world. I know it involves Becky.

The mean spirit is moving through my chest. I become restless. I do not want to give in to what lives in the ashes of my past. Pam had worked hard to put him there, and I did not want to let her down. It wasn't right.

Over forty years ago I survived the war in Vietnam because I became calloused and mean. I was eighteen. I was a killer. I killed to survive. I killed to get even for the death of Americans. I killed because I wanted to. After a while, I killed because I liked to.

I tell no stories about that place.

I carry no good memories, only nightmares.

Truth of the matter is, I survived and came home. For me the hardest part of all was putting the killing down.

The phone rings at noon.

I'm still sitting in my chair, staring at the TV.

A nurse from Good Sam tells me I'm listed as an uncle to Becky Somers. She is in intensive care and is asking for me.

I take flowers to Becky.

She is all doped up and beat to hell. She may never look the same, even after the swelling goes down.

She starts crying when she sees me. "It wasn't Eric," she moans. "His friends did this. His friends…."

I feel a rush of guilt. I can barely look at her.

"Thirty minutes after Eric left for work," she slurs. "They knock on the door and tell me they have something for Eric and want to leave it for him." She sniffles. "I thought everything was okay. Stupid me. I'm afraid Eric will be angry if I don't let them leave his dope. I open the door and they jump me."

I suddenly crave a shot of whiskey. The skin on my back begins to crawl with heat, and rusty nails slide down my throat.

"Just one of them did it. Raped me. He made the other two hold me. He used a beer bottle too, and then he used my mouth." She looks away, embarrassed.

I stare off, burning with anger and guilt.

"Has Eric been to see you?" I ask after a moment.

She nods. "He said he was sorry. So sorry. And he wanted to know if I called you." She sniffles again. Tears on mangled flesh.

I gather myself and study the damage done to her face. It was uncalled for. Any man who would do this to a woman was black with evil in his heart.

She starts nodding out from the dope, and slobbering her words. She goes on to say things that make no sense, things about her life, things about Eric, and then she nods out completely.

I stay with her until the nurse asks me to leave.

"You can come back at nine am," she says.

I glance at my watch. It is nearly four.

I've had nothing to eat all day, but I don't feel hungry.

I stop at the liquor store on my drive home.

I feel awkward buying a bottle of booze. It's been a long time since I've tasted whiskey. Years ago it was my best friend, now I stare at the bottle as though it's a stranger that I don't trust yet.

I know I'm not doing the right thing. I should go to the police and tell them what I know about Becky and Eric and his drug pals. That's what I should do, but I don't.

I have something else in mind.

I'm going to keep my word.

Chapter Eighteen

Faye has her friends over. Other old women with money. I know this by what she's told me about them, and also by what they drive and how they dress. They get together once a week.

It's like a club. They play cards and gossip.

I wonder if Faye is telling them about me.

I don't feel any pride in that.

She doesn't know me. I'm no trophy, that's for sure.

I need to tell her the truth about me. I need to tell her about Becky.

Pam would want me to.

"The truth will burn your heart," is what she used to say. "But you'll be better for it."

I feel that young people don't want to hear the truth now-a-days. They want a distorted version of it. They want what tickles their fancy, fits their life style. They eat the bullshit fed to them by the liberals who think they know what's best for the rest of us, and no one's calling them on it.

It's all a part of the higher learning process.

Trouble is, diversity and political correctness have dumb-downed young Americans with a liberal education, and they are lost in it.

Maybe Steve is right.

America has become a garbage can.

I'm thinking about this stuff while I sit in my easy chair and drink Wild turkey 101. Not a lot, just enough. I'm going to do something tonight that I feel needs to be done. It's important to me.

I put my thoughts to it now, and wait.

Faye's friends leave at eleven. She cleans up. She's a tidy person. It's close to eleven-thirty before her lights go out.

Perfect.

I move out onto the front porch, and sit on the wooden bench that Pam had bought at an antique store downtown.

The bench is hidden from the street by a lilac hedge. We used to sit out here on warm nights and star gaze. She used to hold my hand.

I sip 101 from the bottle. I hold the Dan Wesson in my lap. The night air smells of the river and houses and trees that are thinking of dropping their leaves. I go over my plan as I wait for Eric and he shows up at twelve-twenty, right on time.

He is alone, just as I'd told him to be in the message I'd left on his phone. I'd found his number the same way he'd probably found mine. The phone book.

He parks his Tahoe and climbs out. He looks up at the window while he pulls a baseball bat from the floorboard. He closes his door quietly and crosses the lawn.

My vision is adjusted to the dark.

His is not.

I wait until he reaches the bottom porch step.

"Close enough," I growl.

Eric stops. He is startled. It takes him a moment to recover and bring the bat around in a defensive position.

I lift the .357 from my lap and point it at his chest.

I rasp, "You got five seconds to drop the bat."

"Fucking don't shoot, man. Please don't shoot."

"Drop the bat."

He drops it. I hear it clunk against the porch step.

I smell his sweat and soiled clothing. His eyes are glassy.

I stand and approach him. I feel angry and mean.

"You still want to fuck me up?" I ask.

"Yea, maybe," he says. Losing confidence.

"You need a bat on an old man?"

"What the fuck you want?" he growls. Gaining a little back.

I stare hard at him for a moment. I lower the gun to see if he'll make a move.

He doesn't. Only his lips move, fast and awkward. His tongue darts out and in, wetting his dry lips. His breath is fowl. His eyes jump around like black marbles in a jar.

"I told you not to make it personal, Eric. You laughed because I don't think you understand what I mean. I will kill you. I have killed before. Lot's of times. I've killed better people than you for less than what you've done."

"I'm impressed," he says.

I shrug. "Told you what I'd do if you beat on Becky again."

"I didn't," he rasps. "They went to far, man. I never dreamed they would do that to her. They were supposed to scare her and get her to call you."

"And when I arrived, they were supposed to jump me?"

He nods, losing it again.

"All three of them."

He shuffles his feet.

"And you would be in the clear because you were at work."

He looks away and mumbles, "Yea, man. That was the plan."

"But they went too far. They got carried away like sharks in a frenzy."

"Fucking bastards."

I sigh. "What's on your record, Eric?"

"Huh?"

"You are dodging trouble. Why?"

"I'm on probation. Drugs, and they've got me for a couple other things."

"You love Becky?"

"I used to. We hit it off when I first met her. But she won't have nothing to do with drugs, you know, so that sort of pulled us apart."

"She says she has nowhere to go."

Eric sighs, "Yea, sort of, I guess. Her dad's in prison. Her mother is dead. She has an aunt in Yakama, but she is really religious and Becky's not into that."

I nod.

Eric says, "I want you to know I'll get those fuckers. They were supposed to be my friends. They were supposed to scare her into calling you. Just rough her up a little."

I frown. "Where did you meet them?"

He shakes his head. "The drug world, you know."

"You only know them as a connection to drugs?"

"Yea. But we were tight, you know. We hang out, take care of each other."

I step down close to Eric and hit him with a round house left that knocks him right off his feet and into the flower bed. He goes sprawling across the beauty bark.

I set the Dan Wesson on the porch railing and go after him.

He springs to his feet and squares off with me.

My hands are at my sides. My fists are doubled.

Eric comes straight in, swinging at my face.

I'm slow, but I'm mean and I know right away that I've done this more times than he has. I know it is not the number of punches you throw that wins a fight, but the quality of the few you need.

He hits me three times in the face, but I keep coming. I drive my knee up into his balls, and hit him in the side of his throat. He tries to recover, but I nail him square on the end of his nose. My blows are slow and powerful.

Eric topples over like a duffle bag full of shit.

I pull him up by the collar of his jacket. I slap him four times, two with my palm and two with my knuckles. I turn his hat around, and think about breaking his neck, but I don't. Instead, I turn him around and kick him in the butt as hard as I can. He falls over the lawn, face first. I follow him and pick him up again. I push him toward his Tahoe.

I open his door and stuff him behind the wheel.

"You are a chicken-shit, Eric. You hit women. Only cowards hit women. Becky is off limits to you. Don't go near her again. Got that?"

He mumbles something.

"And tell your drug buddies to stay clear too. I'll kill the son-of-a-bitch that goes near her. You hear me?"

He nods.

Chapter Nineteen

I don't sleep well. Once I drink whiskey and get worked up into anger, I suffer anxiety. I toss and turn. My body wants to shut down, but my mind won't let it.

There are three things I will not tolerate. Abuse, rape and murder. I take them way more serious than some people do. In my opinion they are the last three things our culture has left to stand on, and they are being weakened by judges and politicians who've lost their morals somewhere along the way. But that doesn't mean I have to tolerate them. And I'm only going to say this once, to prey on the helpless is unforgivable in my book.

I could have easily killed Eric, but I didn't.

Why?

Three reasons. The first is logic. As in what do I do with the body? The second is Becky, she still loves that piece of shit. And the third is personal, I do not want to pick up what Pam had suffered so hard to help me put it down.

A year after she is gone, I'm still trying not to disappoint her.

I doubt Eric is counting his lucky stars, but he should be.

My sleep is full of anguish. It's been a long time since I felt this way. I see myself walking away, dangling the gun at my side. I hear a cry for help and the slap of chopper blades.

The gun barrel is smoking.

Nightmares filled with adrenaline make it hard to sleep.

I'm up at five. I make coffee and watch some news. The voices on the TV calm me down. I think about Pam. Her gentleness. I remember the peace I felt when I was with her. I remember how she talked me through bad moments.

I doze off.

The phone wakes me.

I check my watch and see that it is ten-fifteen. Gunshots echo through the room, and I'm not sure where I'm at for a moment.

The room tilts and then sets itself straight. I pick up the phone and rasp a hello.

Faye says, "Hi, Matt. You okay?"

"Yea. I over slept." My head slowly clears.

"You sounded confused. Am I bothering you?"

The prying again.

"No," I rasp. "Just over slept, that's all."

She's quiet.

I wait.

"Still on for tonight, I hope."

"Sure."

"Good. I'm looking forward to it."

"Still want to see a movie?"

"Hum. Think I'm good with dinner."

"Pick you up at seven."

She hesitates. "Sure you're okay."

I nod. I'm thinking I should go see Becky now.

Faye says, "Matt?"

"Yup."

She sighs.

"I have something to tell you tonight," I add quickly.

She says, "Okay. You could come over now and get it out of the way."

I blurt, "No. I have to go somewhere for a while. I'll save it for tonight."

"Okay, Matt."

We hang up. I jump in the shower and I shave.

I check out my face in the mirror. Eric hit me on the chin, over my left eye and on my right cheek. My chin is sore. There is a nice bruise on the cheek, and a small nick over the eye. I can explain them easily. I'm old. Old people hurt themselves all the time. They fall and run into things.

I stumbled into the bathroom last night and ran into the door jamb.

I think about how I was before I met Pam. I used to go to bars and get drunk and pick a fight with the biggest and meanest asshole I could find. In a bar there is always someone to accommodate you. I didn't win all the fights I started, but won my share of them, and most of the time I looked a lot worse than I do now, even when I was the winner.

That morning Pam served me coffee, I was nursing a bad hangover and several fight wounds. I remember how she smiled at me and told me I sort of resembled an angry tom cat who'd taken on a pack of alley dogs and won because I didn't know when I was beaten.

The way she'd said it with her southern accent, still grabs my heart.

I unplug my cell phone and drop it into a pocket of my jacket on my way out. I think about Pam on my ten minute drive to the hospital.

Chapter Twenty

Becky is doing better. Her internal bleeding has stopped. They have removed her from intensive care, and she is not so dopy today.

She smells the flowers I'd brought her yesterday, and she tries to smile, but her lips are to swollen.

"My hero," she says.

I shake my head as I sit down in a chair.

Becky takes my hand and squeezes it.

"You look better," I say.

Tiny teal ripples dart through the green of her eyes. She knows I am just being nice. She knows she may never look as pretty as she was.

I feel bad. Anger pokes at my chest with a dull spike.

"Eric called," she says. "He sent more flowers. He said he can't come to see me right now, but wants me to know how bad he feels about this. He said he didn't have a thing to do with it. He said he will make things right for me, and that he wants to see me again."

Her hand is sweaty. I rub it gently. "You have a lot of healing up to do first," I say, and clear my throat. "Would you ever want to see him again?"

She thinks about it.

I wait.

"We really had something going at first," she says. "It was love, I think. He really is a nice guy when he is not doing drugs. A cop was here this morning. I tried to describe Eric's friends, but I didn't mention Eric. I told the cop they were strangers, knocked on my door and jumped me when I opened it. Pretty much what happened."

I nod.

"Eric was good to me," she continues. "Our love making was okay. He hurries a little. He gets excited…" She giggles.

I smile as I let go of her hand and stand up. I walk to the window and look down at the parking lot.

Becky says, "Right now I don't love, want or have anyone but you, Matt."

I stuff my fat sore hands into my jean pockets. "I'm flattered, Becky, but you know that's not true. You know it will never work between us. I care about you, and you care about me. But we don't love each other. We only used each other. We were both lonesome. It happened, and now we need to move on."

She starts to cry.

I turn to her and watch silent tears slide down her cheeks.

I know that if I go to her now and show sympathy, everything I just told her will have no more impact than a cough in a hurricane.

Becky needs security. Eric let her down, and in a small way, I am letting her down now, but she will get over it.

I let her cry it out.

The truth isn't always as painful as people think.

She smells the flowers again. She slowly wipes away her tears. She gives me a look that says, okay, we have that straight.

I smile and ask her, "Do you want me to contact your aunt in Yakama?"

She shakes her head.

"You need someone to care for you, Becky. I can't do it. Eric isn't capable of it right now, and you have no one else."

She thinks about it. I see it register in her eyes. "How do you know about my mother's sister?"

"Eric told me. He came by last night and we had a talk."

"That's why he won't come here isn't it? You told him not to."

"Not till he's straight," I growl.

She studies my face and notices the bruises and the nick. She shakes her head slightly as she puts it all into place.

"I want to help you. You are going to be under the weather for a while. You need to be with someone who can care for you. Religion won't hurt you, believe me. It will not hurt you one bit."

She closes her eyes and smells the flowers again.

I wait her out.

"If I do this," she says. "You have to promise me something in return."

I think I know what it is, so I nod.

She throws me a curve with, "You have to promise to stop beating Eric up and try to help him."

"He's not worth it," I tell her.

She sighs, "Yes he is. Deal or not?"

I nod, reluctantly.

She looks away.

"What's your aunt's phone number?" I ask.

"I don't know," she says. "You'll have to look her up. It shouldn't be too hard to find her, she is married to the great pastor Daily of the Holy Roller Church in Yakama."

I shake my head at her. I'm thinking my end of the deal will be easy. Once I know she is safe at her aunt's house, I won't have to worry about Eric anymore.

That's what I'm thinking anyway.

I reach into my coat pocket for my charged up cell phone and show it to Becky. "Wow," she says. "Does that big old thing still work?"

"I think so. Been paying the bill on it."

"Does it have caller ID."

"Yup."

She smiles,

"Thought you might want my number. I'm going to be out for a while tonight, and if something happens and you need to get a hold of me."

She reaches her purse and digs for a pen. When she finds one, I give her the number and she writes it down on the back of the card that came with my flowers.

"You should be safe here though," I tell her.

"Think the cops are coming back anyway," she says. "They said they would. Said they need more to go on."

I yawn and say, "You should tell them the truth."

She scowls.

I shrug and think of something else.

"Anyone from the TNT show up yet?" I ask after a moment.

"Yea. Some snoopy bitch showed up early this morning. Must be the one you told me about. She hinted at a connection between you and me. I told her I had no comment."

I rub my forehead.

"What?"

"Nothing," I say. "Hey, you need anything from home?"

"Bottle of Boons Farm wouldn't hurt."

I smile at her.

She reaches out and touches my hand.

A nurse comes in with Becky's afternoon pain killer. She watches Becky take it, checks her temperature and the IV set up. She smiles at me, and I watch her leave.

I'm thinking how pretty and young the nurse is, and how I like the sway of her nice hips in the uniform, when Becky says, "Stay until I fall asleep, okay Matt."

I nod.

"And don't hit on my nurse."

"Just looking."

She smiles and a few minutes later she is sleeping. I stay and watch her for a while.

I think about Pam's last days.

She could have died at home. Our insurance covered a hospice, but Pam told me if she died at home it would be hard on me afterward. "You won't want to use the room. It will always remind you of my passing. Better to use a place you'll never have to go back to."

She died in a different part of this hospital.

I remember the room. It was much like this one, but more convenient for a guest to stay in. The window in her room had a view of a courtyard, crowded with groups of roses. I remember holding Pam and staring at the roses for hours on end. I remember someone telling me I had to let her go so they could take care of her.

I was never supposed to have to come back to this place.

Yet here I am.

And it hurts again, now that I think about it.

Chapter Twenty-one

I'm home at five-thirty.

I change into a pair of slacks and a button down shirt. I brush up my new shoes and comb my hair. I splash on a little Usher cologne, and wait until seven before I walk next door to Faye's house.

She calls for me to come in and have a seat.

I do just that.

She's in her guest bathroom applying the finishing touches to her make-up, I suppose. I hear the bird chirping. I look around her living room and see that she has a computer. I wonder if I should tell her about Becky right away, get her to look up the aunt on that thing. I feel I need to get this out of the way.

But when she comes down the hallway, and I see her, I don't want to do anything to ruin the moment.

Faye is wearing a blue one piece dress that flairs out at the waist and shows a lot of cleavage. She is wearing nylons and heels. She blushes under my stare. She has fixed her hair into curls that bounce along her small shoulders. Her ear rings dangle and sparkle.

She stops and lets out a mild gasp. "Your face. Did you fall?"

"No. I sort of ran into a door."

She moves into my arms and we kiss for a few moments. She is a good kisser, knows how to do it right, and how to gently end it before we skip dinner.

I help her into her coat which has a real fur collar on it.

"Where we going?" she asks.

"Feel like prime rib?"

"Oh yes."

"Was thinking of the Black Angus."

She nods her approval as we step out onto her porch. She locks her door, and takes my arm.

The night is cool and filled with all the smells of fall.

One thing about living downtown during the fair is you have to know the back roads. The Western Washington State fair grounds are right at the bottom of South Hill where the 512 crosses Meridian. A busy location anytime, but nearly impossible to drive through during the fair.

I circle around to Woodland and climb the hill. I turn left on 38th Street, and we arrive at the Black Angus from the west side.

Faye is quiet during the drive. She sits in the center of the seat with her hands folded in her lap. She looks out the window and smiles and once in a while she glances at the side of my face.

After I park, I go around and help her down. She takes my arm as we cross the lot and enter the restaurant. The Black Angus is an ultimate steak house. Plush and clean. Dark enough to feel private, yet light enough to see your way around. Stewart Anderson was a Black Angus cattle rancher from Eastern Washington. He started the Black Angus restaurants, but was bought out of the enterprise by a cooperation. The restaurants used to be called Stewart Anderson's, now they are just called Black Angus.

We luck out again with Faye's request for a booth.

We order the prime rib for two. Faye asks for wine, and I want a pale ale off the tap.. We hold hands and stare at each other while we wait for our orders.

The drinks arrive and while she sips, I gulp.

"What are you thinking, Matt?" she finally whispers.

"How I don't want to spoil the night."

She gently squeezes my hand. "You mentioned something to tell me."

I know it's time, so I tell her everything. I don't try to make Becky look bad, and myself look good. I tell her the truth from start to finish. It took both of us to get into this situation. I watch Faye's eyes as I talk. She is a good listener. No signal. I think she would make a good poker player.

I finish with Becky in the hospital and how I need to find her aunt in Yakama.

I don't say anything about pounding on Eric last night.

Faye lets go of my hands.

I watch her lean back in her chair.

"I'm not proud of my affair," I add. "It's been bothering me. And I was never a hero. It was just a situation I had to do something about."

She nods and then shakes her head.

She thinks about it for a while.

The waitress brings our food.

Faye sips her wine and takes a bite of the prime rib.

I take a big hit off my ale.

She looks straight into my eyes. "My dear Matt. You are such a daring and honest man." She blushes a little.

I can tell she is struggling with something, but I don't suspect it has anything to do with what I've just told her, and I'm right.

"You're not the only one with a skeleton in the closet. You're so honest. Guess that's what I love about you. That, and you're damn handsome."

I down my ale and flag the waitress over for another. I eat some prime rib.

Faye looks away for a moment, and then she says, "Jack is forty-two, married with two children. He works for Microsoft, makes good money. Makes enough to rent a small apartment in Renton that his wife doesn't know about." She pauses and sips her wine. "I was his mistress for several months. I was flattered at first. A man fifteen years younger than me finds me attractive enough to be his lover. He'd call and I'd meet him at the apartment. He bought nice things for me and he was always a gentleman, but after a while I began to feel dirty about our arrangement. It was, after all, only about sex. He was married with two children." She shrugs. "It bothered me to the point of guilt and even shame. So I told him I was not available anymore. It ended ugly."

I nod and eat. I'm thinking she didn't have to tell me about her affair, but she had now, and if her reason was to make me feel better about mine, it had worked.

We eat in silence for a while, and then Faye says, "The most important thing to me, right now, is having someone like you to be with. You're a man's man, Matt. You work on cars. You watch football. You beat people up when you have to. You smell of beer and sweat when you are supposed to. I've been around good looking men all my life, and most of them are only handsome on the outside. Handsome until you get to know them. But you're different. You are handsome on the inside too. You're honest and brave. You're what a smart woman wants. I've watched you and wanted you for a long time. I'm not the least bit bothered by your affair, and I hope you don't think less of me for mine."

"Just so you know," I say. "I sort of like being with you. Knowing about your affair with Jack shows me you had the good sense to do the right thing. I don't think less of you. I think more."

"Oh, Matt," she moans.

The second time with Faye was like pumping propane into a burning house.

She undresses me down to my boxers, kissing me as she does so.

I undress her down to her lacy white panties, and as I become aroused, I get eager and a little clumsy. She giggles.

We take our time, make it last, and it all feels so right.

Later she is lying on top of me. Lamp light the color of oak is playing in her hair. She is staring into my eyes and touching the bruise on my cheek. "Did you really run into a door?"

I think about adding to the lie, but I decide not to. "I had to make sure that Becky is safe," I say. "The person I talked to about it didn't agree at first."

Faye studies my face.

I shrug.

"You would do that, wouldn't you," she whispers.

"When I have to."

She sighs, and I notice something in her eyes that I'm not sure of. Like a subtle hint, it's there and gone in an instant.

I grab her butt.

She smiles.

Chapter Twenty-two

Faye and I have breakfast around eight.

She looks nice in her blue house coat, and she still smells as good as she did last night.

I'm wearing my slacks and shirt with the tails out. I drink coffee and watch Faye move about in her kitchen.

She likes to cook and she is good at it. Scrambled eggs, hash browns, and toast and patty sausage. And she makes a pretty good cup of coffee too, but, I wonder if we are rushing into a relationship. I fear we are filling an empty space in each other's lives that needs filling, but takes time to do so if it is done right.

Faye seems happy, but she doesn't really know me as well as she thinks she does.

I am happy, but I feel there is something out of plumb about us.

I'm suddenly reminded of a piece of advice a good friend at the Veterans Club once told me over a cold beer. "Be friends with your neighbors, but never sleep with one," he'd said. "Problem is. They don't go away as easy as they come, and most of the time they just want something from you anyway."

When all the food is ready and the table is set, we dish up and eat in silence for a while. I nod and grunt my approval while I chase a mouthful with some coffee.

Faye smiles at me over the brim of her cup.

I smile back.

She clears her throat. "You mentioned the girl has an aunt married to a preacher in Yakama. Would you like me to look her up for you?"

"If it's no trouble," I say.

"Not at all," she says as she looks away.

I gaze at the side of her face for a moment. "You feel maybe we're pushing it?"

She shrugs.

"It was a good thing what we did last night."

She blushes and her voice deepens. "Oh yes. Why I'm trying not to push. Don't want to scare you off."

"I'm good with it," I say. "I don't scare easy."

She tosses me a cute little pout.

I wink at her.

After breakfast, Faye fires up her computer and looks up Becky's aunt. It takes about five minutes. She writes down a phone number on a piece of note paper and hands it to me.

"Not positive," she says, "but I think that's the right people. It's an Evangelical church."

"Becky said they were holy rollers," I grin.

"That could be anything but Catholic," Faye says as she rises from her computer.

She walks me to the front door. We kiss and hold each other for a moment, and then I leave.

I'm home alone and it's quiet.

I still like it that way, but I'm thinking Faye's not too bad to have around sometimes. She's not as talkative as I'd thought. I could get used to her, long as it's not a permanent arrangement. That, I don't need or want in my life right now.

I pick up the phone and use it to call the number Faye has jotted down on the notebook paper.

A man answers on the third ring.

I introduce myself and ask if he is the pastor of a church. "I am," he says.

I explain Becky's situation to him. I'm careful. I pick the right words. I tell him I'm a friend. I tell him Becky has no one to turn to except her aunt and I'm wondering if her aunt could be his wife.

He is quiet for a moment, and then he says to me, "I believe she is. Hold on a moment while I get her."

He is gone long enough to repeat all that I've told him to his wife.

When she finally picks up the phone she tosses questions about Becky at me. How bad is she hurt? Where is she at? How long has she been there? Who did this to her? How could anyone do such a thing?

I answer her questions as best I can. Again I'm careful what words I use, and how I structure my answers.

Twenty minutes later, I'm off the phone and thinking it went okay.

I call Becky and tell her it's all set up. "When you get released," I say. "We'll head on over to Yakama."

"Kay," she says. "I'm about to take my bath right now, Matt. Can we talk later?"

"Sure."

By two in the afternoon I'm out in the garage tinkering with the Mustang. I'm listening to classic rock music and thinking about Pam.

I remember our honey moon. We drove out to Ocean Shores and stayed in a dumpy motel that smelled of mold and old furniture. It was all we could afford on my wages at the time.

We didn't even have a view of the ocean.

I'd wanted to give her so much more, and she was so happy with what we had.

Pam could turn mud into sunshine.

We had a bottle of Cold Duck and a bag of Joe Joe's.

And we had each other. We had the rest of our lives together and we really didn't even know each other yet.

Our wedding picture was a four by five glossy that had been taken with a Polaroid by a friend of Pam's. She cherished that picture, bought a frame for it at an antique store and set it on the night stand by her side of the bed.

I'd put it away when she died because it was too painful to look at, but I wondered now if I shouldn't set it out on the night stand again.

I suddenly think I smell Pam in the air around my face.

I turn and look for her in the doorway of the garage. Tears are running down my cheeks.

By four I'm sitting in my easy chair and drinking a beer. I'm staring at the wedding picture as I hold it in my hand. You can't tell that Pam is pregnant in it. She wasn't showing yet. She didn't carry the baby long enough to show before she lost it. And that's when we found out she'd never be able to have one.

She cried for days.

I'm on my third beer by six when Faye calls.

She asks me how the phone call to Yakama went.

"It worked out okay," I say. "Her aunt and uncle seem like nice people. They are concerned. I've made a deal with them. When Becky gets out of the hospital I'm going to drive her over there."

"Oh. Would you like me to come along? We could take my Lincoln, make a couple of days out of it. I'd like you to meet my sister, and I think you'd enjoy her husband."

I hesitate. "Guess that'd be okay."

She's quiet for a moment, and then she asks, "Am I pushing this, Matt?"

I feel she is, a little, but I also feel that I'm enjoying it, so I tell her it's okay. "I'm good with it."

"But maybe we should back off a little," she says. "Let's take a break until we leave for Yakama."

I nod.

"That okay?"

"Sounds fine," I say. "I'll let you know when I know Becky is going to be released, and we'll make our plans from there."

"Oh good. I'll talk to you tomorrow then."

"Yup."

We hang up and I'm about to fetch another beer from the fridge when Becky calls my cell from her room.

She's hysterical. "Eric's friend who raped me got in here. God, he's creepy. He told me I'd better shut my mouth to the cops. He told me he can get to me anytime he wants to, and he'll come again if I rat him out."

I sigh and scratch my forehead.

"Oh, God, Matt." She starts bawling.

I listen to Becky cry and I feel as though I'm swallowing eight penny nails.

The way I see it, Eric is not involved in this. It's the other three acting on their own.

That's the way it shakes out in my thoughts.

They know Becky will call me. They know I'll rush to the hospital. They are waiting. They feel I know too much about the whole situation, and they want to shut me up before I go to the police with their descriptions. The descriptions they allowed me to see the other night when the tall one peed on my fence.

What they don't know is that I have no intentions of going to the police, because to do so would be to reveal the whole story, start to finish, including Becky's lie about my rescue at Duck's store. And what they also don't know, is that I've had enough of their drug games, and I'm ready to put someone down.

I'm sipping whiskey as I drive to the hospital. Good Sam's is at the bottom of South Hill on the east side of Meridian. It's a good size complex spread out with medical facilities and spill over parking across the street from the main entrance. The last two times I'd visited Becky, I used the main parking lot, but this time I park way in back of the spill over lot along the street where the lighting isn't so great.

I take a final hit from the whiskey bottle, stash it in the glove box, and climb out.

I reach behind the seat back and remove the single-nut tire iron from its cradle. It has a sharp edge on the end of its handle for popping off a hubcap. I'd touched it up on the bench grinder in my garage before I left. It's not razor sharp, but it will cut like a knife. I slip the tool up under my Carhart jacket and lock up my Chevy. I'm wearing jeans and a flannel shirt. I'm also wearing a black baseball cap with the bill pulled down low over my eyes.

The night is cool with a drizzle. I smell wet asphalt, the river and soggy trees.

I feel dark, angry and mean as I cross the street and step up on the sidewalk that fronts the main complex. I pass right under the sign that reads Emergency Entrance.

The visitor parking lot by the front entrance is nearly full. I scan windshields until I see the cheery on the end of a lit cigarette. I move left and circle around. I cross over several rows and angle toward the clunker with three shadows moving around inside.

I do not hesitate.

I go straight in.

The tall dark one who pissed on my fence and raped Becky is sitting in the passenger seat. I'm sure he has a weapon in his lap. I'm sure he is thinking about how he is going to take me down.

I imagine their plan was to let me go on in and see Becky.

Once I'm inside they would close the trap.

Three of them milling around, waiting out front in the smoking area. The old man comes out and bang, they close in, pull a gun, and escort him to the clunker for a little ride.

A ride that he might not ever come back from.

Maybe.

I think it's a good possibility because the man who pissed on my fence and did what he did to Becky wouldn't think twice about the next level.

That's on my mind when I bash out his window with the tire iron, grab his head with my left arm and shove the sharp end of the handle into his neck. It would be easy to kill him now. I could do it by ramming the handle into his juggler. Killing is still no big thing to me. Lots of people deserve to die and he is one of them.

But I cut skin and stop.

The one behind the steering wheel with the lit cigarette, and the one in the back seat look about ready to shit their pants.

I see the gun. It's not in his lap, but on the shifting consul, and no one is making a move for it.

All they see in the shadow of my hat brim is my nose and mouth and chin. All they hear is my voice. "Wanna die, asshole."

He makes a gurgling sound.

"I'll kill all three of you. I don't give a fuck."

The driver tosses his hands into the air. "Whoa, no, man. Hey, let's don't go there."

I squeeze the neck a little harder and draw more blood from the cut.

He gurgles at me.

"Leave the girl alone," I growl. "If you ever go near her again. I will kill you. Is that understood?"

The driver and the one in the back seat nod.

The other one gurgles.

I let go of him and walk away.

I take the tire iron back to my truck, and return to the visitor parking lot. The clunker is gone. I enter the building and make it up to Becky's room with an hour of visiting time left.

She is sitting up in her bed. She's reading a People magazine. She puts it down and smiles when I enter.

"Knew you'd come." A tear slides down her cheek. "Did you see him?"

"Yea. He won't be back."

"Thanks, Matt. I told the nurse about him too. If he comes again, they'll call security."

I nod and squeeze her hand before I walk to the window and glance out at the parking lot.

Becky clears her throat and says to my back. "Eric wants me to ask you if he can come see me before you take me to Yakama."

I'm still wound up, but I don't let it show. I shrug.

"What do you think?" she asks.

"You talk to him every day?"

She nods. "He calls before work and during his break."

"You want to see him?"

She thinks for a moment and then she nods slowly.

I'm looking at her in the window. I'm thinking she needs someone other than Eric to take care of her. She is still pale. Her bruises are a deep purple and her cheeks are swollen enough to look as though they have golf balls in them. She looks weak and frail and I want to take her in my arms and hold her.

I turn to her. "If you want to see him, Becky."

She studies me for a moment and I see it click in her eyes. "They were waiting in the parking lot."

"Yea, you might say that," I rasp.

"Oh, God I'm sorry."

"I took care of it."

She looks away.

I stare at the side of her face. "You didn't give the police much to go on, did you?"

She shakes her head.

"Afraid they would involve Eric," I say.

She stares at the floor.

On my drive home, I think about Becky and why she is protecting Eric. She protected him after he pounded on her in Duck's store, and she is protecting him now, even after she'd been raped. I'm not positive, but I doubt she gave the police a good enough description of Eric's friends to lead them anywhere close to the real deal. Her reason is simple. If the police nail them, they have Eric too. He put them up to it to get to me.

They may have went to far, but he is still involved.

Why protect Eric?

Because she still loves him. I've seen the look in her eyes when she talks about how it used to be for them. She misses it. She wants it back. It was as close to a normal life for her, as she's ever had, and she wants it back.

I feel sorry for her.

I also feel that this whole thing is a big mess that needs to end soon.

I reach home and I'm still to wound up for sleep.

I'm sitting on the foot of my bed and holding Pam's wedding ring. The jewelry box is open. I hear the song by Carol King.

I'm replaying what I did at the hospital in my head. It's all very clear to me. The feel of the tire iron in my hand. The sound of the window breaking. The smells of cigarette and dry stale breath.

I feel his greasy hair and sweaty flesh in my hand. I see the trickle of blood.

Bubbles pop in the back of my head.

I could have killed him.

I didn't.

I held up.

Becky doesn't realize how dangerous the situation is becoming for me. She only sees me as her hero.

I'm no hero. I'm just an old man with not much to lose. I try to stay out of people's business. I don't care what they do to themselves with drugs, booze, or even sex.

I have no hard feelings toward anyone because of their problems, unless they cross the line and make them my business.

When I had my problems, I shared them with no one.

In bars when I tried to pick fights. The people I picked on always had the right to say no. Once in a while one of them would, and I respected his decision and moved on. As I've said, I'm no saint, but I've always honored another human's rights to walk away.

Way I see it, Eric and his pals give up those rights by their actions.

The tall one who peed on my fence may or may not know how close he came to dying tonight. I'm glad he didn't. I'm glad I held up.

I'm also glad that Becky has agreed to go stay with her aunt.

I'm thinking these problems will go away once she is in Yakama. I'm hoping I never see her or Eric and his friends again.

I want to move on. I'm going to do the right thing for Becky and then do my best to wash my hands of it all.

Sounds like a lot of wishful thinking, don't it.

Chapter Twenty-three

Becky is released from the hospital on Saturday morning. Faye and I drive over to Good Sam's and pick her up in Faye's 2012 Crown Victoria. I'm driving, and Faye is talking about the weather.

"It's unseasonable warm out," she says. "We're having an Indian summer. Nice for the fair. Have you been yet?"

"No," I say. "Was thinking about skipping it this year."

We've allowed our relationship to cool off for a couple days.

I went to my weekly dinner with the Veterans, and she went out shopping with her friends. I worked on the Mustang, and she worked in her garden.

We talked on the phone and we waved at each other over the fence.

I visited Becky nearly every day, and Faye always asked me how she was doing.

When I told her they were going to release Becky on Saturday, she asked if I still wanted her to come along. She really wants to see her sister, and thinks I might enjoy her brother-in-law who refurbishes old cars and sells them for a living.

I told her I'd like her to come along and that we'd make the weekend out of it.

Faye was thrilled, and she still is. "Maybe when we get back from Yakama," she says. "We'll take in the fair one night. I like to go on weeknights. It's a little less crowded."

I agree, but don't say anything.

I'm thinking about the deal I'd made with Becky's aunt. I wasn't so sure about it all just yet. The aunt was concerned, but didn't sound too enthused about having her long lost niece as a guest. No, she couldn't come and pick her up because she was the music director and would miss practice, but yes, she would look after her while she healed up, if I'd drive her over to Yakama.

When I called her yesterday to let her know we were coming, she didn't sound all that jubilant.

I clear my throat and say, "I'm a little worried about Becky's aunt and uncle. I'm not sure how this is going to play out."

"I know how I would feel if it were my niece," says Faye, "Why would you worry?"

I told her about yesterday's phone call and my take on it.

"It will be okay," she says. "Surly it will work out.

I hope she's right. I move my thoughts to Becky, and how she was having second thoughts about the arrangement too. It seemed as though the healthier she became, the more she tried to back out of the deal.

Yesterday she said, "She'll smear me with religion."

"And you'll be better for it," I'd replied.

"How would you know?"

"Trust me on this."

I don't think she does, but I'm not giving her a choice.

Becky's standing out front of the hospital when we arrive.

I introduce them as I help Becky into the huge back seat.

Becky says to Faye, "Nice to meet you. I like your car."

And Faye says, "I've heard a lot about you and I'm glad to finally meet you."

Eric had brought a suitcase full of Becky's cloths to the hospital yesterday. I loaded it into the big trunk next to Faye's small suitcase and my overnight bag, and then I climb in.

The drive is quiet for the first hour of it.

Becky is unhappy, and Faye is uncomfortable.

I use the quiet to think about Eric's friends and our little meeting in the hospital parking lot the other night.

I don't think it's over yet. I may have stopped them from messing with Becky, but I have a feeling they are still hanging around with Eric. He's a chicken shit. A man with balls would have gotten even. If she were my girl, I would have killed the man who raped her, but that's the difference between my generation and the ones coming up. In my opinion, Eric is the epitome of coming generations in America. They all wanted change. They voted for change and they got it, but I want no part of it.

I can remember when the slogan used to be, "Love it or leave it."

Now it's become, "If you don't love it, we'll change it for you."

Remember when our motto was, "Ask not what your country can do for you, but what you can do for your country"?

Sort of makes you sad, don't it?

Anyway, I'm thinking about this stuff as I drive, and I'm thinking I will probably have to deal with Eric's friends again, whether I want to or not, and I'm also thinking how it's sort of strange to be driving a car with the last two women I've slept with as passengers.

I wonder why I'm doing this, and I think it's because it's the right thing to do for Becky, and I also think I might be using Faye to distance myself from what I'm ashamed of.

And then I stop thinking, and just drive.

It is a three hour trip from Puyallup to Yakama, and it is a beautiful fall day. I take highway eighteen to Interstate ninety, and go straight on up over Snoqualmie Pass. The trees are in full color now, I see smears of amber, yellow and red mixed into the evergreens. The Doug Firs are huge and they grow close to the side of the road.

Faye is clad in tight fitting designer blue jeans, a yellow blouse and a leather jacket. She is dolled up and smells of an expensive perfume. She breaks the hour long silence when she stares at the side of my face and says to me, "I like having someone drive who knows how to handle a car like this."

"I like this car," I say. "It's heavy and stays on the road. I like leather seats and big engines."

She smiles.

Becky says, "Would you guys stop that shit."

Faye rolls her eyes.

I glance at Becky in the rearview mirror and she mimes gagging on her index finger. I shake my head at her, and she frowns. I can't help but feel sorry for her. She looks a little better, but still has the appearance of someone who was stuffed into an oil drum and rolled off a cliff. She's puffy and bruised and scarred.

I put my attention back on the road and think about how pretty she was, and then I feel angry and I wonder if I shouldn't have ripped the man's throat out with the tire wrench.

Could I kill again?

Hell, I don't know. It's not something I want to think about. So I think about Becky's reaction when I'd told her about Faye a couple days ago when I'd paid her a visit in her room, and she'd asked me to walk with her out in the court yard where the roses are.

"You're more comfortable dating someone closer to your own age?" she'd asked.

"I am."

"Is she pretty?"

I nodded.

"Bet her butt checks and boobs have slumped."

"She has taken pretty good care of herself."

Becky thought about it for a moment and then she said, "You're a pretty good looking old man, Matt. And you're sort of mucho in a natural way. Lots of women would love to have you dating them."

I shrugged.

"How long have you known this Faye woman?"

"She's lived next door for a long time, maybe ten or twelve years."

"Did your wife like her?"

"They got along."

"She flirted with you, didn't she?"

I tossed her a scowl. "I'd rather not talk about it."

Becky said after a moment of thought, "I'd be careful."

"Should have been more careful with you," I shot back.

"But I've always been honest with you. You've always known what I'm about, and our relationship."

She took my arm.

"That's sort of true," I said.

"Think Faye wants something from you."

"You don't even know her," I growled.

"Kay," she said and squeezed my arm.

I glance at Faye now, and wonder about our relationship. I feel we're being fairly smart and honest about it. I still feel something is a little out of plumb with us, but I don't agree what Becky or Sylva on the matter. I believe it is something else. Most likely something very small.

We stop at a Shell in Ellensburg for gas.

Becky is sleeping. I'd seen her take a couple of pain pills a little while ago.

Faye climbs out and goes inside the store to use the restroom. She comes back with two cups of coffee and a bag of white donuts.

I finish filling up the big tank and enter the store. I pay for the gas with cash, and I use the restroom.

I have only one credit card. I use it only in situations where one is required, such as checking into a major hotel. Pam burned all of our other credit cards years ago. It is one of the methods she used to save us money.

Once we are back on the road, I catch Highway 82 which splits off of I-90 and runs over three barren peaks on the way to Yakama.

The country is dry on the eastern side of the Cascades. Most people think of Washington State as rainy and green because of the Seattle, Tacoma area. That is where the majority of the people live and it does rain a lot.

The eastern side of the state, however, is dry and arid. Winters are cold and summers are hot. It is beef, corn and wheat country. Black Angus and hay fields. Not a lot of people, until you reach Spokane or the Yakama wine valley.

The coffee Faye bought for us is hot and strong. The doughnuts are sweet and messy.

She breaks into my thoughts by clearing her throat, and then she tells me about her mother, who passed away several years ago. She was a true cowgirl. She rode horses and herded cattle, and mended fences and lived on a ranch all her life. She was originally from Pasco. She married a rodeo stock contractor. She knew no other life, but allowed her two daughters to venture out and find their own peace.

I realize how comfortable I feel with Faye when she's talking.

I like the way she rambles on, and never doubts that I'm listening. I feel I might be getting used to it. Maybe.

Pam had talkative moments, but mostly she was quiet. She liked to sit close to me and touch my hand. She liked to stare at my face. She liked to look out the window while we drove.

I miss the silence we shared together.

It was always peaceful. It was as though we shared moments together in our thoughts.

I know in my heart that Pam wants me to move on.

I feel she would approve of Faye.

I think she would tell me to give it try, why not.

Faye suddenly reaches over and squeezes my hand. I glance at her and smile.

She asks, "You still concerned about it?"

I glance into the rear view mirror and see that Becky is still asleep. I nod at Faye, and she asks, "Is there a plan B?"

"No. I don't know what I'll do if this doesn't work."

She looks thoughtful.

I add, "I just want her to be safe."

"How about the police," says Faye. "They couldn't locate the men who did this to her?"

"I don't think they had much to go on."

"Did they ever question you?"

I shake my head.

"Maybe you should take the whole story to them."

That's an idea I'd sort of tossed around a couple times in the last couple days. I'm not crazy about it, but it is a possible solution to the problem.

Faye adds, "All of them belong in jail, including her boyfriend. She'd be safe then."

I nod.

I am fairly neutral in my feelings toward the police. I think most cops do their best to serve and protect, but their hands are tied by criminal lawyers and liberal judges. I remember hearing a story on Fox News about a woman who was raped in Denver Colorado. Her assailant was arrested and released. He made it home before she did.

The police in America have to walk on eggshells when they make an arrest. That's not the way it was intended to be, but it is, and it seems to me that the police don't really stop crimes anymore, then just try to arrest the people who commit them, and that's a big enough task in itself.

No wonder I hesitate on taking my story to them.

I glance at Faye and rasp, "I guess that will be plan B."

She smiles and nods. She thinks she is being helpful.

Little does she know about me.

Chapter Twenty-four

We reach Yakama in three hours and four minutes.

Faye uses her cell phone to find the address I'd jotted down on a piece of notebook paper. She tells me what exit to take and exactly how many miles it is to the church.

Becky wakes up and pops another pain pill. I glance at her in the rearview mirror. Her eyes are glassy and her hair is tangled from sleep.

I ask her, "How you feeling?"

She shrugs at me in the mirror.

It takes us about fifteen minutes to find the church and the small white house behind it. The church building is not as large as I'd thought it would be. It is built of brick and lined with stained glass windows down both sides. The steeple does not have a bell in it. The little white house behind the church is a rambler. It looks well kept. The yard and flower beds are maintained. Not a weed in sight.

I park in the driveway. Faye and I climb out and stretch. Becky crawls out of the back seat and stares at the church for a moment, and then she says to me, "If this turns out bad, I'll never forgive you."

I smile at her and she turns away.

Her aunt and uncle come out of the house, and they look to be nice people to me. He is wearing blue jeans and a flannel shirt. She is wearing a long cotton dress under a button down sweater. They look wholesome and strong. Their eyes are clear and they have that way about them that all Christians have when they know for a fact they are going to Heaven. It's a peace that you can see in their eyes.

Becky's aunt is small and slender with green eyes and short blond hair. Her uncle is not much taller than the aunt. He has brown hair and brown eyes.

I open the trunk and remove Becky's bag.

We introduce ourselves. Handshakes all around. Becky gets a big hug from her aunt, but her uncle only gives her a gentle shoulder squeeze.

Several awkward moments pass, and then the aunt says, "How about some coffee and lunch."

"Well thank you," I say, "but we need to be on our way."

She holds me with a little smile and replies, "Thank you for bringing her over." And then she glances at her husband.

"I would like to have a word in private with Mister Conner," he announces. "If that's okay."

I nod and try not to look surprised.

The aunt, who knows what's coming, takes Becky by the arm, and says to Faye. "Let's us girls go inside. I'll show Becky her room, and we'll get her settled in."

Becky rushes over, gives me a hug and whispers, "Remember your promise." And then she swings away.

Faye is caught off guard, but she recovers quickly. She tosses me a curious look, and then she follows Becky and her aunt into the house.

I'm wearing blue jeans and a button down shirt under a lined windbreaker. I stuff my hands into the pockets of the windbreaker and gaze directly into Pastor Daily's eyes.

He folds his arms and returns my gaze. "I would like to apologize for the reluctance on our end, and any inconvenience it may have caused you," he says.

"No problem," I say. "I'm retired. I have a lot of free time."

"I take it you and Mrs. Evans are close friends."

"Neighbors," I answer and I see where he is going with this, and I'm suddenly very happy I brought Faye along.

"And in what capacity do you know Becky?" he shoots back.

It hits me like a brick. The good pastor and his wife have been doing some thinking. I guess I don't blame them. If it were me, I'd want to know more about myself and my relationship with Becky too. I know his concern is genuine, but I don't like being treated as a sinner about to confess his darkest sins.

Once again, my rig manager's training kicks in. The art of interrogation and the deception of answers. I keep my voice level as I say, "Obviously, I know her well enough to be concerned about her. Becky lives in my neighborhood. I met her at the corner store. She actually had someone try to mug her in the store. I was there, and I stopped the mugging. We've kept in touch, but it hasn't been that long. Maybe two weeks."

I watch him absorb my answer.

I decide to give him some more. "Becky lives with a young man named Eric Swanson. He is a welder at a fabrication shop in Fife. He's into drugs. He was not directly involved in Becky's assault, but his life style may have contributed to it. I don't think he's good for Becky. Why I wanted to get her away. I realize she's a grown woman, but she's still young enough to be my daughter."

He nods and asks, "Was it a lot of trouble talking Becky into coming here?"

"Not at all," I lie.

He studies the ground for a moment.

I say, "I understand your concern. I'm a total stranger."

"We've tried talking her into coming over several times through the years," he says thoughtfully. "She has always refused our help. My wife has feared something like this would happen. Now it has." He clears his throat and tosses me a look that tells me he doesn't believe everything is as I've said.

I'm fine with that, but I have a question of my own, and I ask it with dignity. "I was a little surprised you folks didn't come get her, rather than wait for me to bring her. Is there going to be a problem with her staying here?"

He turns a little red as he replies. "No. Not at all. We were just a little concerned about the situation. We've suspected Becky might be involved with drugs, to be honest, and then we get a phone call from a total stranger, and..." He shrugs.

I give him the hard nod of understanding, and we shake hands.

"Thank you," he says.

"You're welcome."

A moment later, Faye and Becky's aunt appear on the small front porch. They are smiling and talking. They hug briefly and then Faye comes toward us.

By the grin on her face, I figure her interrogation went as well as mine did.

"God bless," calls Pastor Daly as we climb into the big Lincoln.

We wave at him. He grabs Becky's suitcase and turns away.

Faye is quiet until we are five minutes down the road, and then she chuckles and says, "That sweet woman raked me over the coals."

"About us?"

"About you and her niece."

"In front of Becky?"

She shakes her head. "That girl nodded out before her aunt could get the pillows fluffed."

I smile. "Sorry I got you into this."

Faye shrugs. "I don't mind. I had fun playing the innocent neighbor who was asked to help out."

"You made me look good, I take it."

"Not a hard thing to do, Matt."

I shake my head.

She pats me on the arm.

I ask, "So what's your take? This going to work out for Becky?"

Faye thinks about that for a moment. "Probably. They'll smother her with religion, and it will be good for her."

"Becky doesn't think so."

"She will someday. That girl is troubled right now, and she is headed down a road that will only lead to more misery. She will jump from one wife beater to the next. Her tires have fallen into a deep rut and she can't figure out how to climb out of it. We've just given her a little push."

I glance at Faye. "How do you know these things?"

She shrugs. "Sounds about right, doesn't it."

I figure it does, but I'd thought maybe she'd read a magazine article about battered young women, or watched a program on television about them.

I don't know if I've given Becky a little shove from the rut, but I know she needs to stay away from Eric and his friends for a while, and I also know religion won't hurt her.

Faye's sister lives five miles out of town on several acres facing the Yakama River. The house and shop buildings are clustered along a gravel driveway. Grape vines grow along both sides of the road, and the hillside behind the place is covered with grape vines as well.

It is twelve-thirty when we arrive, and they are expecting us because Faye had called and set it all up.

The three dogs are Shelties. They race over and bark at us while I park. We climb out and stretch. The dogs circle us and continue barking, until Tom, Faye's brother-in-law, tells them to hush.

We do the introductions, handshakes and hugs out on the driveway.

Faye's sister is an older version of Faye, with blond hair and a big butt. Her husband is tall, grey and thin, and he doesn't say much. He doesn't have to because Faye's sister talks more than Faye does.

A couple minutes later, they usher us inside.

Their house is big and airy. The floors are all tile and hardwood. A massive fire place stands in the center of it as though it were built first and then the rest of the house around it. Granite counter tops are everywhere, even in the bathrooms. The place reeks of money.

After a quick tour of it, we have lunch in the shade of their veranda which looks out over the grape vines and the Yakama River.

The air is cool and crisp with fall. It smells of the country and cold water, and of the late harvest grapes, which according to Faye's sister make the best wine of all.

The lunch is chicken salad and French bread and wine.

The girls talk continuously. They talk about everything from recipes to relatives. They stop to smile and giggle once in a while, catch some air and sip some wine, and then one of them takes up the next subject.

They don't even seem to notice when Tom and I leave.

He tosses me a shy grin and pokes his thumb toward the French doors.

I nod and rise from the table. Tom leads the way inside and back through the house. Our shoes click on the marble tiles as we reach the foyer.

"Faye mentioned you are interested in old cars," he says.

"I am," I reply. "I have a '73 Mach One that I tinker with. It was a retirement project. I'm not much on refurbishing, but I like old cars."

He says, "We'd better hurry if you want to see a few of mine."

I give him a puzzled look.

"The sisters will be fighting before long," he adds.

"They seem happy to me," I say.

"You'll see," he says. "Give them about thirty minutes."

The Shelties are snoozing on the front porch when we step outside. They bark and wag their tails and follow us down the steps.

We walk down to the outbuildings. Our shoes crunch on the tight packed gravel. The dogs circle us and bark once in a while. Tom angles over to the largest of the three buildings, and lets us in through a man door on the side of it.

"Where I do most of my work," he says, and turns on the lights.

I'm immediately impressed.

Tom has a nice set up. It's obvious he enjoys doing what he does, and he is very good at it. He tells me he drives back to Minnesota, North Dakota and New Mexico once a year and buys cars. He has a large lowboy trailer that he pulls with a Chevy one ton dually.

Most of his cars are early to late fifties, but he has some from the sixties and seventies as well. They are at various stages of refurbishment. A couple are ready for paint, some are about half way, and some are only stripped down.

"Out along the I-40 in New Mexico," he says, "where the old route 66 used to run, is a good place to find these cars, and also up north alone the highway going into Farmington."

"Where do you get your parts?" I ask.

"Mostly on line, but I like to hit the junk yards once in a while."

"You do everything yourself."

He smiles and nods. "The building straight across the driveway is my paint shop, and the one next to us it my engine shop. I've got a small Extend-a-boom for pulling the motors. I paint with air."

I gaze around like a child in a candy store, and we get lost in conversation. We talk cars. Engines, chasses, transmissions, frame and body designs. Tom knows way more than I do, but he's not arrogant about it. He's polite, and more than willing to share his knowledge with me.

It is maybe thirty-two minutes later, when Faye comes waltzing in to the big shop bay and asks me if I'm ready to leave.

Tom smiles.

"I guess so," I tell her.

"Well let's head out then," she spats and turns and leaves.

"Thanks, Tom," I say, and we shake hands.

"Give me a call if you need a part for your Mustang. I can get it for way less than most people."

"I will," I say and I follow Faye out the door.

Chapter Twenty-five

Faye and I drive back over to Ellensburg. She wants to get away from her sister. She tells me she will feel better with three mountains separating them.

That's all she says. She doesn't talk about it. She just sits and looks out the window as we climb the three barren peaks. Only sounds I hear is the slip of wind over the contours of the Lincoln, and the gentle hum of tires on asphalt.

I like the quiet. I don't know what ruined Faye's day, but mine is still fine, and as we fly along the highway, I gaze out at the rugged terrain and allow my thoughts to absorb the colors I see.

Somewhere around eighteen-thousand people live in Ellensburg. It is the county seat of Kittitas County which contains the Kittitas Valley which is internationally known for its timothy-hay. There's a college here too. And the town being centrally located in the state once made a bid to be the capitol, but lost out to Olympia, which is much closer to Seattle and Tacoma where the majority of the people live.

Ellensburg leans toward supporting Democrats. It went to Obama in 2008, but I don't hold that against it. It's a pretty town in the shadow of mountains, with a lot of old buildings to look at. Ninetieth Century buildings. It has a nice park on the Yakama River, and ten hotels to accommodate travelers.

I drive us around for a while. We take in the sights and enjoy the smell of the fall air and the dying leaves. I stop at a Texaco and top off the fuel tank. I drive to a Safeway about two blocks down the street, and while I pick up a six pack of Henry's pale ale, Faye grabs a bottle of late harvest wine from Columbia Crest.

She is feeling better by the time I check us into a Holiday Inn Express. We ride an elevator up to our room with our bags. I let us in with a key-card, and while Faye freshens up in the bathroom, I sit on the bed and use the remote to find a college football game. I have to settle for an ugly one, but its better than watching golf or bike racing. I am kicked back and half way through my first Henry's when Faye reappears.

She takes the ice bucket and fetches some ice from the vending area down the hallway. She places the bottle of late harvest in it and sets it on the dresser next to the television.

She's all smiles as she plops down on the bed next to me. She snuggles and puts her head on my shoulder. She gazes at the TV, and falls asleep within minutes.

I smell her hair and her perfume and I think about Sylva and Becky's opinions of her. I wonder what they perceive that I don't. I also wonder why so many college football games are so lopsided. After a while, I doze off.

I wake Faye around seven when I crawl off the bed to use the bathroom.

She yawns and asks, "You ready for dinner?"

"You bet," I call as I close the door.

A couple minutes later, I'm sitting on the foot of the bed watching Faye fix the flat spots she'd put in her hair while she slept. She uses a round brush and a dab of water.

"You enjoyed Tom?" she asks.

"Yup."

"Figured you would."

I nod, thinking I could have spent the rest of the day with him and never felt bored.

Faye looks at me in the mirror. She says, "Sorry I was so rude when we left. And for not being good company on the drive over."

I smile. "I'm okay with it."

She turns from the mirror. "You like the quiet, don't you."

I nod.

She turns back to the mirror and puts the brush down.

I say, "Like the quiet, but it's nice to have someone with me in it sometimes."

She tosses me a smile and picks up her purse from the dresser.

Faye takes my arm as we walk to a steak house down the street. We are early enough to get a booth with a window view of the Cascade Mountains. I order an ESB off the tap, and Faye has a glass of blush wine. I also order a well done rib-eye, with a salad and a baked potato. Faye wants her rib-eye medium. We both ask for blue cheese dressing on our salads.

The drinks arrive and I'm enjoying my ale when Faye reaches across the table and touches my hand.

"Matt," she sighs. "Do you find me attractive?"

I nod. "Sure I do."

"Do you think I'm only after money?"

"My money?"

She nods.

I laugh.

She looks down at her wine. "My sister told me to stop being a gold digger and look for someone to love and settle down with. Like she's got it so great with greasy old Tom."

I didn't think Tom was greasy, but I say nothing.

Faye lifts her eyes to mine. "The more I'm with you, the more I realize there is so much about you that I don't know."

"Not missing much," I say.

"My sister thought you were very handsome. I think she is jealous."

I think her sister is happy with what she has, but I don't say anything.

Faye says, "I've told you so much about my life. Would you mind telling me about yours?"

I do mind, but I sip my ale and say, "I have a brother in Portland, without Pam, he is about all I have left for family. Our mom past away when I was in Vietnam. Our dad past away when we were kids. Dean is a year younger than me. I pretty much took care of him while Mom worked."

"You're close to Dean?"

"I was until I went away to Vietnam."

"My high school sweetheart died in that war," she says. "Rumor had it he died within ten minutes of his first firefight. When the Moving Wall came to Seattle, I visited it. Found his name. It was odd staring at his name after so many years. I wept. Didn't think I would, but I did." She pauses a moment, and then she adds, "Mostly I think because I felt his death was senseless."

I nod and look for our waitress, hoping a break in the conversation will change the subject.

I see her and wave her over. She's young and pretty. She is wearing tight jeans and a western shirt. Her hair is auburn and her eyes are blue. She hurries over and lays a smile on me that makes me want to give her a hug.

I ask for a refill on my ale. Faye downs her wine and does the same.

Our waitress swings away.

Faye gazes out the window, and I think about Pam and how I never truly felt I was home from Vietnam until she entered my life. She loved me enough to ride a barbed wire rowboat into hell if that's what it took to bring me back. And believe me, sometimes my anger and guilt pushed me pretty darn close to the gates of that place.

Our food arrives right after the drink refills, and we dive into our salads.

Faye asks thoughtfully, "How did you lose your father?"

"We don't talk about it," I reply. "He died and left us nothing. That's how I remember him. Oh, and he liked to fish."

She smiles.

I shrug.

She asks, "Why were you no longer close to your brother after Vietnam?"

I think about that. I decide to be honest, yet evasive. "War changes everything, especially when you are still just a kid. You grow up fast in war, and you discover things about life that you probably don't need to know until you get old, and maybe not even then. I was too different to relate to my little brother anymore."

She accepts that for an answer and we eat in silence for a while.

I'm half way through my steak before she says, "My high school sweetheart, the one who died in Vietnam, told me the night before he left that he was not coming back. I thought he was just saying that to make me feel I had to put out for him, but turned out he was right. What is it about you men and your wars, Matt?"

"I don't know," I say, "and my hunch is not worth repeating."

She reaches across the table and touches my hand. "Maybe someday you'll tell me your hunch," she whispers.

I nod to be polite, but there is no way I'll ever tell her my hunch.

When we return to the room, the wine is chilled enough to drink. Faye pours two plastic cups full of it, and we sit on the foot of the bed. I'm not much on wine, but this stuff is pretty darn good. Not too sweet and not too dry.

Faye says, "Do you like it?"

I nod.

She sighs and looks down at her feet. "Did you enjoy the sex you had with Becky?"

I'm a little startled. I'm thinking good heavens, Faye, what happened to slowly directing a conversation where you want it to go, so the other person has a chance to think about their answers.

"It was okay," I say after some thought. "I'm not proud of our relationship. I always had a feeling of guilt, and I think that might have gotten in the way a little."

She nods. "I never felt guilty with Jack, but I never felt completely satisfied either. I think I was trying to feel younger, and it didn't work."

I'm not sure what to say next, so I say nothing.

Faye tosses off her wine and moves to the dresser where she refills her cup. She turns and leans on the dresser. She tips the cup to her mouth and gazes at me over the rim.

I smile.

She takes down the wine quickly and sets the empty cup down. I see the promise of something special suddenly fill her eyes as she removes her blouse and jeans. She takes her time removing her bra. Her breasts have a nice lift to them when her nipples are hard. She leaves her small white panties on.

She approaches me, and I suddenly feel all knotted up in my chest. She kneels and unzips my pants. I take my shirt off, and shiver. I allow her to do what it is that she wants to do, and I hope she is not doing this because she thinks she needs to out-do Becky. I struggle with that notion for a moment, and then I realize it feels too good to care, so I let it go, and when I'm close to the boiling point, I reach out and pull her on top of me.

We are exhausted afterward.

Faye cuddles and falls asleep without a word.

I lie awake for a while. I wish things were different. I wish Silva had never planted the seeds of doubt about Faye in me. I hope she's wrong. I also hope Becky is wrong. I hope

Faye and I hit it off for a good while. I like her company. I like the way she makes me feel, and I think Pam approves of us.

But I don't think our relationship will last long. I feel that Faye thinks she knows me, and she doesn't. She only knows the lonely man who lost his wife a year ago. She doesn't know the other side of me. She's never seen the other mood.

I'm also beginning to think that Becky may have been partially right. Faye does want something from me. It's just a feeling, but it's pretty strong. All this special treatment has to lead us somewhere. She's no rooky at this. She's been around the horn and had to putt from the rough a few times.

She wants something, and it's not just companionship.

It's something else.

I feel our relationship is headed toward it.

I only hope Faye doesn't get hurt.

I'm not worried about myself.

Hell, I'm good to go.

It is cloudy and cool in the morning.

Faye and I check out at eight and we decide to enjoy the free breakfast before we leave. They have it set up buffet style in the restaurant. We join the small crowd. I heap my plate with scrambled eggs and link sausages. I pour a cup of coffee and a glass of orange juice. Faye selects coffee and toast with a small yogurt.

All the booths are taken. Faye picks out a small table with two chairs in a far corner of the room. Private and quiet. We settle in and I start to eat, but she sips her coffee and stares at her toast.

She'd been solemn all morning. She was up and in the shower when I woke, and she was dressed and ready to go when she came out of the bathroom. I took a quick shower and I didn't shave. Faye seemed eager to be out of here. I didn't want to hold us up. I wonder if she is having second thoughts about last night. Maybe she needed time to come to terms with it, and the sooner we were on the road, the easier it would be for her.

I try to think of something to say, but I'm not sure if I should say anything, so I eat and sip my coffee and think about how much I had enjoyed last night, and how I didn't feel the least bit guilty about it, and I'm replaying some of it in my head when Faye lifts her eyes to mine.

"You okay?" I ask as I try to read her.

She nods.

"You look nice," I say.

"You've never seen me without make-up," she tosses back.

"I didn't know you ever wore any."

She chuckles and shakes her head at me.

Once we are out on the I-90, I set the cruise control on seventy and I glance at Faye. She is quiet. Her hands are folded in her lap, and she gazes out the window.

I decide to leave her alone.

I like the quiet anyway. I like the sound of air slipping past the window. I like the soft hiss of the tires on the road. I start to think about Becky. I wonder how her first night went. I wonder how she is getting along with her aunt and uncle.

Suddenly Faye asks, "Matt, was it good?"

"The breakfast?"

She rolls her eyes. "You know what I mean."

"Yes. It was good."

She glances at the side of my face. "You enjoyed it?"

"Oh yea."

She blushes as she stares down at her hands in her lap, and she says, "Being with you makes me feel like doing things I haven't done in a long time, Matt. I don't know what got into me last night. I don't want you to think I'm that way. Does that make sense?"

I nod as I think about the virtues of our generation before the sexual revolution.

She looks at me.

"I don't think less of you," I say. "If that's what you're worried about."

"It's just not my style."

"I know that."

She looks away.

I say, "I'm sorry if I gave you the impression I wanted you to do something you were not comfortable doing."

She shrugs.

"Hope I didn't."

"It's not that," she says.

I don't know what else to say, so I drive and think about it. I've never asked a woman to do anything she doesn't want to do. I've always been happy with whatever a woman is willing to give. With Pam, it was always up to her, and thinking about it now, hurts, so I move my thoughts back to Faye and I think I know why she is so bothered by what she did last night.

I don't remember that sort of sex being common when I was in high school. Most girls back then cared about their reputation. The ones that didn't may have gotten more dates, but not many marriage proposals.

It's an old way of life I still remember, and Faye does too, and I think she may feel her virtues are damaged, now, and I played a role in it.

Maybe she'd had too much wine and I should have stopped her. Or maybe I should have made a bigger deal out of it afterwards.

Thanked her or something.

I don't know. I've never been able to read women.

I couldn't even read Pam after forty plus years of being married to her.

I let it go and drive and I think about Becky again, and I remember something she said about our relationship. It had something to do with honesty, and to me that also means knowing where a person is coming from. It is true that I knew what Becky wanted. Love and security.

Do I truly know that much about Faye?

I sigh and figure that's enough thinking about women, and move my thoughts to football and beer.

We reach Snoqualmie Pass around eleven and it is raining on the west side of the mountains.

No surprise there.

I slowdown in preparation for the sharp wet turns ahead.

Faye says, "Funny how I grew up on the dry side of the state, but feel more at home on the wet side now."

I glance at her. She tosses me a smile to let me know she's feeling better.

"There's something about the rain," I say. "I grew up in it and never seemed to notice. It never stopped me from doing anything I wanted to do."

"I know what you mean," she says. "Growing up around Mosses Lake, I used to think it rained in Seattle and Tacoma every day. But after I lived in the Puget Sound area for a while I realized that it rains a lot, but it is nice a lot of times to, and when it is nice, it is really nice."

"Only drawback," I say, "is the moss on my back. It's hard to scrub off some times."

"And your webbed feet make you a little clumsy," adds Faye.

We smile at each other.

"I'm sorry about my mood this morning," she says.

"I'm good with it."

She studies the side of my face for a moment, and then she asks, "You ever been over to Ocean Shores and stayed at the Indian Casino?"

I shake my head.

"We should go sometime. It's a lot of fun."

"I'm not much on gambling."

"Neither am I, but you don't have to gamble. There are other things to do."

I shrug.

"My friends and I, we girls, go about twice a year, and stay a couple of days at the casino. I'm not sure what we are really looking for, mostly just a good time I think, and once in a while we meet older gentlemen with money who wine and dine us. Nothing serious ever happens. It's harmless fun." She pauses, and then she says, "But there was the one time, when something serious did happen." She stares at her folded hands in her lap.

I wait her out.

"That's how I met Jack," she sighs. "It was one of the rare times we went on a weekend. It's always so crowded on weekends, but anyway, we were there, and Jack's company had some sort of team building event going on, and one evening while I was playing a slot, he suddenly took the one next to mine, and--no need reliving what happened from there."

I suddenly have light air in my chest. I glance at Faye, but she continues to stare at her hands. I look back at the road.

She says, "I was flattered that a man his age would be attracted to me. I imagined it to be a one night deal for him. And I was willing to be a part of it. Why not. My friends were sick with envy. Nothing serious would come of it." She starts crying silently. She opens her purse and removes a tissue. She dabs at her tears. She drops the sun visor down and uses the little mirror on the flipside of it to check her mascara.

I feel sorry for her, but I don't know if I should. I have the feeling she's not finished with this story, and my involvement is coming next.

She shakes her head. "It ended ugly, I've told you that. Happened months ago, but he's suddenly started calling me again. I've explained to him about you, and that I'm not interested, but he doesn't seem to believe me."

I suddenly feel I may have dumped one problem in Yakama, but I've been carrying the other one with me all along. I don't want to think Faye would use me, but I have to wonder about it.

She gazes at the side of my face. "He knows where I live."

I drive and say nothing.

She reaches over and rests a hand on my thigh. She leaves it there the rest of the drive home.

I park Faye's big car in its space at one pm straight up. I carry her suitcase to her door and set it down. She takes hold of my arms and looks into my eyes.

I can tell she wants me to say something about her situation with Jack, but I'm not going to. I need to think about it for a while. I need to let it cook in my thoughts and see what develops.

She pouts, gives me a kiss, and let's go of my arms.

I turn and start to leave.

"Can I bring dinner over at six," she calls as I go down the steps on her porch.

"Sounds good," I say. I figure I'll have had a little time to think about her Jack problem by then. Right now, I don't care.

It is beer and football day.

I cross the yard, carrying my small bag and thinking about watching the NFL on FOX the rest of the afternoon. I climb the steps to my porch and unlock the door.

Someone had paid me a visit.

Chapter Twenty-six

Faye brings a small dinner over at six. I'm sitting in my slashed up easy chair with Pam's empty jewelry box in my lap.

Faye gasps at the mess they made. "Matt, have you called the police?"

"No," I mumble.

"You really should, Matt."

I look at her. "I know who did this."

"All the more reason to call the police."

I rise from the easy chair and shake my head.

Faye asks, "You think Becky's boyfriend was involved?"

I start to pick things up.

It took me three days to put my house in order. Some things were broken beyond repair and I had to throw them out. Pam's computer and my TV were two of them. My bed had been peed on. My clothing had been peed on. My walls had been peed on.

Not a lot of things were missing. Just small things they could hawk in a hurry, like Pam's jewelry, her digital camera, and her coin collection. They destroyed more than they took.

They didn't get my guns. I thought that was ironic, but when I considered how busy they were smashing things and peeing on them, they probably didn't spend a lot of time searching the closets. It would have taken them some time to find the guns anyway. I keep the pistols under a box of ceramic tiles we had left over when we renewed the kitchen floor, and I keep the shotgun behind a false door deep in back of the closet.

My floors are all old hardwood. Cleaning them wasn't too difficult, but my mattress and bedding, among other things, had to be replaced.

Faye was over several times. She helped with a lot of the cleaning. She never mentioned calling the police again, but she hinted at it a couple of times, and after I didn't respond, she dropped it. She helped me find a new easy chair, a TV, a mattress and bedding, and a few other items that needed replacing. All in all, they didn't do a good job of burglarizing my home. I felt they more intended to leave me a message than anything else. A message that I would not easily forget. A message I read loud and clear.

The key was missing from the back porch. That was how they'd gotten in, and if I'd been home at the time, I'd be hamburger right now. I went up to Home Depot and bought a new lock set. I won't leave a key out under a flower pot anymore, I can guarantee you that.

On Wednesday I'd call Clark and told him I'm not going to make it for lunch. I didn't want to lie, so I didn't give him a reason at all.

He told me Steve had already called and informed him he had a doctor appointment. "Probably his blood pressure," he said. "We'll shoot for next week."

I told him that sounds good and we hung up.

In the afternoon on Thursday, I decide to tinker with the Mustang. Eric and his pals had not broken into the garage. It was untouched. I probably have a couple thousand dollars' worth of tools in my box, not to mention the damage they could have done to the Mustang.

As I said before, they didn't do a good job of burglarizing, because this was more about the message.

I shake my head as I turn on the radio and lean into the engine compartment. They are playing "Cinnamon Girl" by Neil Young. I stare at the four barrel Holly carburetor and think about Pam, and I suddenly tremble with anger. My world tilts slightly, and shadows slide across the walls. My head fills with sound….

A train rushes by out on the tracks beyond the alley. I glance out the small window and see that it is evening. I have no idea where my mind has been the last few hours, and I don't give a shit either.

I close the hood on the Mustang, put my tools away and shut the lid on my box. I lock the garage door as I leave.

I'm in the kitchen when the phone rings.

Faye says, "Matt, I've been trying to reach you. Did you go for a walk or something?"

"Naw. Been working on the Mustang in the garage. Lost track of time, I guess."

"Want company? I've made a small dinner."

"Ate a late lunch," I lie. "Not really hungry tonight."

"You okay, Matt?" she asks.

"Yea. Tired. Think I'll go to bed early."

"Was thinking that myself." Her voice slips into a husky whisper.

I say nothing. I'm not trying to be rude, I just feel moody, and filled with broodings.

She sighs. "Well maybe we'll do lunch tomorrow."

"Sounds good," I say.

"Night, Matt."

I say goodnight and set the receiver down.

I sit alone in my new easy chair which is similar to the old one, but not as comfortable, and I'm watching Thursday Night Football on my new forty-two inch TV. I have Pam's empty music-jewelry box in my lap, my loaded .357, and a cold can of Ice House beer.

The music box won't play anymore.

They broke it, must have smashed it against the floor after they emptied it.

I have tears in my eyes as I think about how Pam used to open the box sometimes just to hear it play. She didn't have a lot of jewelry, just what I'd given her through the years, and I wasn't much on shopping for things of value, but I bought her what I thought she might like, and she always treated every one of them as though they were the most precious things in the world.

The wedding ring had cost us three-hundred dollars which was a lot of money to us at the time. Before Pam died, she'd removed it and put it in the box. She'd told me to get it out and squeeze it whenever the anger boiled up inside me and tried to take control of my actions. She'd also told me to bring it along when I joined her in the hereafter.

My actions.

I don't want revenge.

I do not want to get even.

I just want my life, and Pam's wedding ring back. I've paid the price for my sins. I've faced up to what I had coming. The playing field is level. Pam had no part in this. She did nothing to deserve this.

I think about calling the police.

I could tell them the whole story, start to finish. I could tell them where Eric lives and works. Eric will lead them to the other three.

What can cops do?

By now, everything's been hawked off.

How hard will the cops work to get the ring back?

Good chance things will only get worse if I involve them.

Good chance the police will only go after the drugs.

I'll have to identify Eric and the one who likes to pee on everything. I'll have to identify the other two.

I shake my head. I stare at the gun. I know what I must do.

I take a big gulp of beer and wipe away the tears.

It's time to answer their message.

I have personal reasons now. They made it that way.

Chapter Twenty-seven

I'm sitting in my truck and drinking whiskey. Not too much. Small sips that burn all the way down.

Good old Wild Turkey 101. The liquor store was my first stop. Eric's house was my second.

I'm parked up the street from it now. I can see Becky's car in his driveway, and I have a good view of his front porch. My .357 is on the seat next to me. I'm listening to a classic rock station on the radio. They are playing "Time" by Pink Floyd.

It is nearly midnight.

I know Eric gets off at eleven. He should be home any minute unless he stops for a beer. I hope he is alone. I hope he does not have a weapon. I do not want to shoot it out with Eric. I do not want to beat him up again. I only want the ring back. If he cannot get the ring for me, then everything changes.

I see Eric's Tahoe coming up the street from the opposite direction. I had guessed right. I'd figured he'd drive through Fife and take River Road home.

I watch him park in his driveway. He parks right next to Becky's Toyota. He gets out and carries a lunch bucket into his house. The lunch bucket is a small green and white cooler. I wonder how many times Becky cleaned it and packed it for him. I wonder if he ever told her thank you. I wonder if he carries drugs in it.

I climb out of my truck and stuff the .357 into my coat pocket. I'm wearing the Carhart, the same one I was wearing when I met Becky. The pockets are deep. The gun slips right in. I check to make sure it also slips right out.

It does.

I walk down the street and straight up to Eric's house. I figure a man like him, living in a neighborhood like this, probably doesn't lock his front door right away. This is a quiet neighborhood, just as mine is. Blue collar people. The real middle class. The cost of living didn't bring anybody's wages up, it just expanded the size of the middle class. People making over a hundred thousand a year really don't have much more than the people making less than that. They just have newer things and maybe nicer things, but they still live from check to check and still spend their fair share at Walmart and Fred Myer.

We all live the same dream and lock our doors before we go to bed.

Eric is a drug addict though. He might be paranoid. It's a chance I'll take.

I reach his front door and turn the knob.

The door opens and I enter to find Eric sitting on his couch.

He is drinking a beer and watching one of the late shows.

He sees me and panics. He drops the beer and leaps to his feet.

I'm afraid he is going to draw a weapon.

His eyes are as big as quarters and he breaks into a sweat.

I slip the gun out and point it at his chest. I draw the hammer back even though it is double acting. "Sit down," I growl.

"What the fuck. Don't shoot, man. What the fuck?"

"Sit down."

He plops down. The couch is old and worn. The cushion sags beneath him.

"I want the ring," I say.

"What ring?"

"The wedding ring you stole from my wife's jewelry box."

"I didn't take it. I didn't do it."

"You were with them."

"But I didn't take anything. I was there to get even with you, man. That's all. I didn't take anything. I swear."

I kick the front door shut. I reach back and lock it. I do this for two reasons. The first one being I don't want Eric's drug buddies to come up behind me without any warning. The second to punctuate my presence in Eric's house. To make a statement. "It's just the two of us."

He starts squirming now. His eyes dart around the room and he is licking his dry lips.

I smell his sweat and the old furniture.

I feel high on the whiskey. I feel mean. I feel numb. I know I can blow Eric away without remorse. But I also know that Pam wouldn't approve of it. She would not approve of what I'm doing. She would want me to let them have the ring. It would hurt her, but she would look at it as a material possession not worth fighting for.

She's also not here anymore.

"I want the ring, Eric. If you don't have it, find out who does and get it for me. I'll give you one day."

He gives me a nervous laugh. "It don't work that way, old man. You are crazy. That ring is long gone by now."

"What do you mean?"

"It's been sold."

"Who sold it?"

"One of my pals."

"Thought they weren't your pals after what they did to Becky. You told me you were going to get those fuckers."

He looks away.

"You're a chicken shit, know that."

"You don't understand the situation," he says, and shakes his head. "You don't mess with people like them. They will kill you and leave you in an alley somewhere. They don't hesitate, and they are pissed at you for what you did at the hospital."

I think about that for a moment.

Eric adds, "They told me they were sorry they went to far with Becky. I don't have much choice but to let it go."

"How'd you know about the key on the back porch?"

He thinks and then he says, "Same way you knew my door wasn't locked yet, I guess. The way Becky could come and go, I figured there was a spare."

I nod. "Who took the ring?"

He shakes his head.

"Same guy likes to pee everywhere?"

"Maybe."

"What's his name?"

"He goes by several."

"What do you call him?"

"Jackknife."

I think about that, and then I notice the small green and white cooler next to Eric's feet. I wonder why he didn't carry it into the kitchen and set it down on the table or the counter top. He obviously went straight to the fridge for a beer, but he kept the cooler with him.

"What's in the cooler?" I ask.

I see the lie forming in his eyes right away. The pupils get bigger and darker. A bead of sweat rolls down his forehead. He shrugs and answers me without looking at the cooler. That way he makes it a small thing. "What's left of my lunch," he says.

"Becky use to make good lunches for you?" I ask.

"Yea. She's a good cook. She use to make good meals for me and she always packed me a good lunch."

"You miss her I'll bet."

"Yea."

"Get up and back off, Eric."

"Don't do this, man," he says.

"What?"

"You know what I'm talking about. You don't want to do this. You will get both of us killed, man. I'm serious."

"I want the ring, Eric."

"I promise I'll try to get the ring back for you. But don't take the lunch bucket."

"You work with someone who deals, don't you?"

"Maybe."

"What time are they supposed to be here to pick up the shit?"

"I don't know. They don't keep a schedule. Could drop by any minute."

"Okay. We'll wait."

"Are you fucking crazy, man? Jackknife will kill both of us."

"Then get up and back away from the cooler."

"I can't just let you have it."

I knew what he meant. I also knew he deserved whatever they did to him because of the way he'd done Becky, but for some reason, I liked Eric just a little bit. I didn't want him damaged too bad for Becky's sake, because I believed she would come back to him some day.

She was like that. I had that much of her figured out..

Eric says, "You may as well kill me as take the cooler, or be here when they get here. Either way they are going to fuck me and you up. This is big shit…."

He was still talking when I hit him. The distance was five to seven feet. I covered it reasonable fast for my age, and busted Eric's head open with the .357. I hit him hard enough to knock his lights out for a few minutes. Long enough for me to grab the cooler and leave.

I was shaking when I climbed into my Chevy truck. I was shaking when I fumbled out the key and started her up. I took two quick hits off the whiskey bottle and they calmed me. I drove home knowing that I'd made it personal with them to.

Good.

I needed a plan now. I needed to stay on top of this. I needed to remember what kind of people I was dealing with and what they might do. Eric is a coward and a dumb-ass. Jackknife isn't, and I don't know about the other two.

Chapter Twenty-eight

I t is nearly two when they arrive.

I'm waiting in the heavy shadows of the bushes that divide my front yard from Dick and Silva's. I'm holding my Smith and Wesson twelve gauge. It has a barely legal barrel on it and it is staggered loaded with four slugs and three double ought.

My eyes are adjusted to the dark. I am stoned on whiskey. I feel mean and angry enough to kill. I don't care anymore.

They idle up in the Dodge clunker with the busted passenger window. They kill the headlights, but leave the engine running. The four of them high on dope and alcohol. They stare up at my dark house. The driver's window is open. I watch him turn and say something to the one in the back seat behind him. He opens his door and puts a leg out. He is five feet away. I leap toward him, and slam the door on his leg pinning him right there. I shove the barrel of my shotgun behind the driver's ear. The one with his leg trapped cries out. The rest of them freeze. Eric is in the back seat on the far side. He's holding a baggy of ice on his head. He cowers down. Jackknife is the front passenger. He glares at me, and I make good eye contact with him as I growl, "If you don't have the ring, put this heap in drive and disappear until you do."

"Fuck you, old man," says Jackknife. "Give us our dope."

"When I get the ring."

He scowls. "You don't know who you're fucking with."

The one with the trapped leg has pain tears rolling down his cheeks. He shoves on the door, and I push harder. "Christ," he moans.

"The ring," I say to Jackknife as I glance at the scab on his neck.

"You're dead," he replies.

The driver puts the clunker in gear and starts to roll forward. I let go of the door. The one in back pulls his leg in and closes it. Eric stares at me through the back window as they drive away.

Jackknife was wrong.

I knew exactly who I was fucking with, and I wasn't done.

You can say what you want to about George Bush, but he had one thing right. Once you identify your enemy, you take the fight to them.

Exactly.

I climb into my Chevy truck and fire her up. I idle away from the curb and follow the clunker at a good distance. I figure they are not going very far from the dope. I also figure they are going to regroup and come up with a plan on how to take me out and get it back.

They drive to Eric's house, park the clunker in the driveway next to Eric's Tahoe, and right behind Becky's Toyota. They go inside. One of them is limping. Two of them are armed. Eric is shaking his head and I figure by now he is wishing he'd have never gotten involved with these people.

I think about a couple of things I can do to mess with them, but I stay in my truck. I wonder if they are telling the truth about the ring and if I should let it go. I'm tired and need sleep. I'm angry, but not stupid. I want to mess with them, make them suffer a little, but I wonder if they are worth it. I don't want a war, I'm too old for that. I suddenly feel foolish about all this and drive away.

Chapter Twenty-nine

The phone wakes me at eight-thirty.

I'm sleeping in my easy chair with the shotgun gun. My head is pounding, and my throat feels as dry as the state of Arizona. I croak a hello into the phone.

"All right, old man, I'll tell you where the ring is."

I know it isn't Eric. I'm thinking it's Jackknife, but I'm not sure.

I say nothing.

He continues with, "You listening. Don't die on me."

"I hear you."

"Ok. There is a jewelry store run by a rag-head out on South Tacoma Way. It's called Pay-Less Jewels, or some fucking thing. He didn't give me much for the ring. It ain't worth much. And as of this morning, he still has it."

"Then go get it," I say.

"Don't piss me off, old man."

"Don't fuck with me, Jackknife."

He pauses and breathes heavily into the phone.

I wait him out.

"Ok. But I gotta sell some of the dope in order to have the money to buy the ring back."

I am sort of ready for that, and I reply with, "Eric works, borrow the money from him."

"Have you looked in the lunch bucket?"

"No."

"About eight grand worth of product in there. You are denying a lot of people their candy, old man. How's about I start telling them where it's at."

"How's about I just give it to the police and tell them where I found it."

"I'm going to kill you."

"I want the ring, Eric."

"It's gone, man. I hawked it. It's long fucking gone. Who knows where it's at by now? Some whore could be wearing it. What part of all this don't you understand."

I redden with anger. "I understand all of it. And you better start picking up whores until you find the one wearing the ring, or you'll never see the dope."

"You're dead. You are a dead son-of-a-bitch, old man."

He hangs up.

I put the phone down, rise from my chair and go make some coffee in the kitchen. I think about what Jackknife said, and decide to open the ice chest and see what's in it. While the coffee starts to brew, I retrieve it from the coat closet and carry it into the kitchen. I set it down on the small table and slide the lid open. There are six large freezer bags of yellowish-white powder inside. I have no idea if this is eight thousand dollars' worth, but I know if it is, then there might be someone more powerful, smarter and probably meaner than Eric and his three pals involved in this.

He's the one I don't know who I am fucking with.

He is also the reason I need to give the cooler back to Eric and forget the whole thing.

Losing Pam's ring hurts badly, but I'm not going to die over it.

I pick up the phone in the kitchen and dial Eric's number.

Jackknife answers. "Yea."

"Know what my truck looks like?"

"Is this you, old man?"

"Yea. Know what my truck looks like, right?"

"That junky Ford missing a tailgate."

"It's a Chevy."

"Whatever, man, what's your point?"

"You'll see me drive by Eric's house in five minutes. The cooler will be on the end of his driveway. Don't come out and get it till I'm gone."

"Your lucky day, old man. You came to your senses before we really fucked you up."

I sigh. "I want this to be over with, Jackknife. I don't ever want to see you or hear from you again. We clear on that?"

"Maybe."

"No maybe. It's over."

"It's over when I say so."

"You want the dope?"

He hesitates. "Okay. Give me the cooler, and if everything's still in it, it's over."

I hang up and grab my coat. I'm nearly out the door when Faye calls.

"Matt," she says when I answer. "Still on for lunch?"

"Sure. I have to run an errand, and I'll be right back. Wanna go up the hill?"

"Was thinking about some teriyaki. Nice place on River Road."

"Sounds good. I'll pick you up around eleven-thirty."

"You okay, Matt? You sound, upset."

"I'm fine."

We hang up and I take the cooler out to my truck. It was more like eight minutes to Eric's house with the phone interruption. I stop up the street, and study the place. There is a cool light drizzle falling. I have my window cracked a little. The air smells of wet houses, lawns and shrubs.

I see no movement at all, and all three vehicles are in the driveway.

I ease forward and stop. I see Jackknife and Eric staring through the picture window at me. Eric looks worried. Jackknife is smiling.

I leave my truck in drive and hold it with the brake. I open my door and drop the cooler. It tips to one side and slides across the wet pavement as I pull away. I glance in my rearview mirror and watch the driver of the clunker snatch up the cooler and trot off to the house. He must have been hiding behind one of the vehicles in the driveway. My hands are sweaty and shaking. I speed up.

Chapter Thirty

Happy Teriyaki sits down by the river in an older shopping area. The old K-Mart is called a Circle K now, and what used to be the Hi-Ho shopping center is now a strip mall that includes a barber shop.

Faye is wearing a light grey pants suit that fits her tight across the butt. She is wearing heels, and a long rain coat. She looks and smells nice.

I'm showered and shaved. I'm wearing a clean pair of Lee jeans and my new shoes. I'm wearing a cotton sweater under my Old Navy winter coat. Pam had bought the coat for me a couple of years ago. It is probably what they call dated, but I don't give a shit. I like the coat. It's warm and it fits.

I feel better. I know I've done the right thing.

Pam would approve.

When I go to her and explain why I don't have the ring, she'll smile and nod.

That's how she was, and will still be when I go to meet her. The most forgiving person I've ever met.

I want to close the Becky/Eric portion of my life and get on with it. I want to enjoy Faye's company, and work on her problem. I want things to return to normal. I want to sleep in my bed again, and wake up without a whiskey hammer in the center of my forehead.

I order the sweet and sour pork, and Faye asks for the almond chicken. We both order ice tea with our meals, and while we wait, Faye updates me on her friend who is about to marry a younger man.

"She's pretty certain he wants her money," she says, "but he is just so damn cute and he makes her feel so wonderful. She is, however, thinking about having him sign a pre-marriage agreement."

"So if it don't work out," I say, "he will only get so much of her money."

"Probably none of it," she says.

"Then he probably won't marry her."

"What she wants to find out."

I shake my head.

Faye says, "The rest of us have a bet. I'm saying he does marry her."

I toss her a curious look.

She smiles. "There are ways of getting to the money once they are married. I've talked with a good lawyer on the matter."

I wonder why she would do that, but I don't ask.

She says, "The way things are now-a-days, Matt, there are a couple of things he can do to get some of her money even with the agreement."

Our food arrives and we start to eat.

I wonder if Faye's friend, the one about to marry a younger man, hasn't consulted a good lawyer too. I also wonder why she would bother marrying the kid if she is so certain he is after her money. Being the type of low intelligence person that I am, I can only conclude that he must be hung like a wagon tongue.

Faye interrupts my thoughts when she says, "Jack called this morning. He wants to have lunch and talk about what happened."

I swallow some pork and chase it with ice tea.

Faye studies my face for a moment, and then she adds, "I told him I would discuss it with you."

I shake my head. "I'm not really a part of it. I have no opinion because I have no idea what you mean by ending ugly. Did he get rough with you?"

"A little. My arms were bruised."

"He scared you."

She nods. "Most of our fight was verbal. He said some things that he shouldn't have said, and so did I. But you know how it is. If you said something vicious, even though you didn't mean to, the thought was in your heart somewhere all along."

Pam and I had never fought, so I have no idea what it would be like to argue with a woman, but I do understand what Faye means by the last part.

She looks away as she says, "He called me a whore, Matt. That's when I tried to leave. He grabbed my arms and squeezed a little too tight."

"Are you afraid of him?" I ask.

"He's not really a violent person. No, I'm not."

"But you want to close the book on that part of your life."

She nods. "It was ugly."

"You think he wants to start over."

"Why else would he want to have lunch? I don't want to see him again. I want him to leave me alone."

"You've told him that?"

"Yes. I've told him all about you, and our relationship. It doesn't seem to faze him. He rattles on about how much he misses me, his marriage is on the rocks because of me, and he's drinking more than he should. Like he's trying to make me feel guilty about it."

I'm thinking I don't need any of this mess. I have no idea what to tell Faye, and I also have no idea what she wants me to do, but I tell her what I think she should do. "Meet him somewhere for lunch, Faye. Maybe if you tell him to his face, he'll get the picture."

She is a little startled by my suggestion, but she recovers and after some thought she asks, "Will you come with me?"

"I don't know. Maybe I shouldn't," I mumble.

She reaches across the table and grabs my hand.

"Wouldn't that be awkward?" I ask.

She is looking into my eyes.

We are back home by three. I walk Faye to her door, and as I'm about to leave, she grabs me and we kiss. A big kiss, and then she bats her eyes and says, "Will you think about it, Matt?"

I nod as I try to read her eyes, but as I've said before, Faye would make a good poker player.

"I know it sounds crazy," she adds. "But I don't want to meet him alone."

"I understand," I lie. "We'll talk about it later."

She kisses me one more time, and then I go down the steps on her porch and walk over to my house.

I change clothes and check the mail for bills.

I take the garbage out from under the sink and put it in the can out by the gravel alley. I enter the garage, I turn on the Mustang's radio, pick up a 7/16" box end wrench and lean into the engine compartment.

They are playing "The Joker" by Steve Miller, and I see Pam in tight jeans and a cotton shirt. She is standing by a baggage claim carousel at SeaTac. I am walking toward her. She sees me and smiles. She always made my homecomings seem special. She was beautiful. She never needed make up, and rarely wore any. Her nose was small and pointy. Her cheek bones were narrow, her mouth was wide. In tight jeans, her legs looked nine miles long. She was slim with full breasts, and a round butt.

I loved the sway of her hips when she walked toward me. The way she held me with her blue eyes still pounds a nail in my heart.

My eyes dampen with the memories of how she used to make me feel as though I were the best thing going in her life every time I stepped off the plane.

By six I'm in the easy chair and watching Fox News. The president is calling the scandals phony. I'm thinking there is more proof of their existence than not of it, but I really don't care. America is getting just what she deserves.

The phone rings and I think it's Faye inviting me over for dinner, but it's Autumn. "Hello, Matt."

"Hi. How are you doing?"

"Good, and you?"

"Been busy. A little more than usual."

She says, "I take it that's why you haven't called me."

I say nothing.

She says, "Well, are you still interested?"

I hesitate. Faye comes to mine, along with her problem, and I hear myself saying, "Yes." And I'm thinking it would be nice to date a woman who doesn't have a problem, or need me to do anything for her, and doesn't live in the neighborhood.

"How about next Wednesday? Meet me at The Olive Garden on the hill for lunch?."

"Sounds good."

"I'll call and remind you Tuesday night," she says.

"Okay. I'm looking forward to it."

We say goodbye and hang up.

Five minutes later, I'm still thinking about Autumn when Faye calls and says she's bringing dinner over.

By seven-thirty we are sitting at my dining room table and enjoying a chicken and pasta casserole with wine. Faye is telling me about her sister. She'd called to apologize, and they were on speaking terms again. Her sister was impressed by me and is hoping Faye has finally found someone to be happy with.

I'm wondering why she is telling me this.

She suddenly goes quiet.

I don't know what to say.

She looks into my eyes and I smile.

"Matt," she says. "Am I pushing?"

"Pushing what?"

"Us. You know. Matt."

I shrug and say, "I like what we have and what we do."

"But are we moving too fast?"

I think about it for a moment. "Life is fast, Faye. Way I see it, at my age you don't turn down the good things. The things that make you feel happy and good about yourself. Before you and I started seeing each other, I was awful lonely and depressed. Now, I ain't so bad off."

She absorbs that while we eat in silence for a moment, and then she asks, "Have you thought anymore about the lunch?"

"The one with Jack?"

She nods.

I hadn't really, and I don't remember telling her I would, but I have an answer. "If he agrees to it, sure. I'll go with you."

She lifts her wine glass and says "Good. That will make me feel so much better."

"Think he'll go for that?"

She sips her wine. "He won't have much choice if he wants to talk."

I'm thinking if he wants to talk about rejuvenating their relationship, he won't want a third party listening in. That's absurd. The guy's got too much at stake. I don't see him agreeing, which leads me to believe that Faye has something else in play here, and I'm not sure if I want to be a part of it.

After dinner, Faye washes the dishes and places them on the drying rack. I grab an Ice House from the fridge and sit at the table watching her.

Pam and I had never bought a dishwasher because Pam didn't want one. She enjoyed doing dishes the old fashioned way. I used to watch her just as I am watching Faye now, and I realize how important a woman is in a man's life.

It's the things they do. I can think of no other way to put it.

When Faye is finished with the dishes, she pours another glass of wine and brings it to the table. She is wearing a light blue skirt and a yellow cotton blouse. She sits and folds her legs and after a sip of wine she asks, "Want me to stay, Matt?"

I nod.

She blushes slightly, and I'm aroused.

I wake at two.

I wonder why.

I remove Faye's hand from my chest and crawl out of bed. I put my underwear on and a pair of blue jeans. I slip into a flannel shirt, but I don't button it up.

It is cold in the house. I hear the rain tapping on the shingles. I hear it rolling down the eaves and dripping into the gutters. I hear a gust of wind come up and move through the bushes in my front yard. I do not know why, but I walk into the guest room and stand at the window.

A car is parked out on the street.

Not a late model Tahoe. Not a Dodge clunker.

A large black car, maybe a Crown Vic. It is shiny and slick with rain. It is parked just out of the glow of the pole light. All the windows are tinted. I see no shapes or shadows from inside. It seems to wait long enough for me to have a good look, and then it slowly glides away and disappears.

I stare out at the rain falling into the dark. I have a feeling I know what that car is all about. I go down stairs and check my guns. I check the locks on the doors, and I go back to bed.

It seems as though hours pass before I sleep again. I hear Faye's heavy breathing, and I think about her problem. I think she wants me to go with her when she has lunch with Jack, because if I don't, she is afraid she'll say yes to him and be right back where she was a few months ago. Jack is probably good looking and one hell of a lover. Way I see it, Faye wants a more permanent relationship, maybe even marriage, and Jack can't do that, or he won't.

I'm no prize, but I'll do to keep around for a while.

I think Faye started our relationship with good intentions. I believe she is attracted to me for the reasons she has stated. I also think she is in love with Jack, but she doesn't want to admit it, even to herself. I believe she wants Jack to dump his wife for her, and he's not going to do that.

That's how I see it.

Faye and I are not in love.

No one is going to get hurt.

With that decided, I move my thoughts to the big black car. It can only mean one thing. My problem with Eric and is pals is not over yet.

I suddenly feel beads of sweat on my forehead, and something like a rusty nail in my throat.

Faye says, "Coffee and oatmeal sound okay with you?"

"Sure," I say.

She is standing at the side of the bed in her bra and panties. She is holding one of my flannel shirts. "Do you mind?"

"No."

She puts the shirt on and it reaches just below her butt cheeks. She heads down stairs and enters the kitchen. A few minutes later I smell coffee brewing. I get up and use the bathroom before I dress and descend the stairs.

Faye and I sit at the table and drink coffee while the oatmeal cooks. It's in a pot on one of the stove burners. A pot and a burner that haven't been used since I lost Pam. That feels odd, but I deal with it and gaze at Faye.

She looks nice with her hair full of sleep tangles.

I tell her the coffee is good, even though it is much weaker than I drink it, and it doesn't have brown sugar or condensed milk in it.

She yawns and I smell sleep and coffee on her breath.

I think about Pam and how she always brushed her teeth first thing every morning. She always kissed me over our first cup of coffee, and I remember how she tasted.

Faye kicks my leg.

I look into her eyes.

"You okay with this?" she asks.

"Sure," I say.

She sips her coffee and says, "What's in your plans today?"

"Saturday, I don't know. Guess I don't have any plans."

"How about we hang out together."

I feel something tighten up a little in my chest, and I look surprised.

"I have nothing else planned," she adds.

I nod.

"Well? What do you think?"

I'm thinking I want to be alone, and away from her and her problem. I sort of like our come and go arrangement. I try to be careful when I say, "Maybe we shouldn't do that yet."

She eyes me with a coolness that I'd not seen in her before.

I sip my coffee and look away.

She asks, "What are you afraid of, Matt?"

"It's not fear," I say. "It's more a matter of not being ready."

"I've asked you if I'm pushing it. You've said its okay."

I look at her.

She holds me with a look that's cold as glacier water.

"Okay," I say. "Here's the deal. I'm attracted to you and it's not just the sex either. I like being with you. I like hearing you talk. You're fun to be with. I've said that before and it's all true. I'm just not ready for a full time deal yet. I need space. I like it quiet sometimes. I wanna go tinker with my Mustang today, what are you going to do while I'm doing that? I want to drink beer and watch college football. Does that sound enjoyable to you?"

"Those things are part of a routine," she says. "You can't break your routine once in a while? Even one day, for me?"

"Guess not," I reply.

She looks away while she absorbs my answer, and then she shrugs and rises from her chair. "I'm going home," she spats.

I watch her leave the kitchen. I hear her climb the stairs and enter the bed room. There's a silent space of maybe two minutes while she dresses. I hear her come down the stairs, open my front door and leave.

I'm alone, and it is quiet.

I like it, but I think I smell oatmeal burning.

A couple hours later I'm in the garage. The oatmeal was pretty darn good for being over cooked. I'd put some butter on it, and brown sugar. I'd also had a couple pieces of toast with it. I'm good with the toaster and I'm good with the microwave.

Other than that, I'm fairly lame in the kitchen, which leads me to the reason I eat a good share when I'm out with someone, which prompts me to think about Faye and our disagreement this morning.

But I'm not going to deal with that here in the garage.

This is where I connect with Pam.

I'm not going to allow anyone to take that away from me. Not now, not ever.

So I turn on the radio and I hear the song "Fresh Air" by Quick Silver, and I grin as I open the hood on the Mustang, pick up a wrench and lean in.

I remember the time Pam and I almost bought a dog. We were on one of our Sunday drives out by Eatonville, and there was a kid parked along the road with a small dog and a sign that read, "Pup for Sale."

Pam begged me to pull over, and I did.

The kid was maybe eighteen years old. He was dressed in bell bottom jeans and a flannel shirt. His hair was blond and stringy. His eyes were blood-shot blue. He sat on the tail gate of an old Dodge truck and he had the dog tied to the bumper with a piece of sash cord. He wanted twenty dollars for him. He was a four month old Red-bone and Walker mix hound. He had long legs and big feet and floppy ears. Not to mention sad green eyes which Pam fell in love with immediately.

She knelt and began to play with him while I talked to the kid.

He told me he lived on a commune just down the road a ways. They'd had a meeting last night and decided the dog had to go. "He got into the chicken coop," added the kid. "He's not a bad dog, still a pup. Just mischievous, that's all. Only reason I need twenty dollars is 'cause that's what I paid for him. Don't really want to let him go."

"What's his name?" asked Pam.

"I call him Bogart because he hogs his food, but he'll answer to most anything."

She studied the kid for a moment, and asked, "Which you gonna do if you don't sell him?"

"I haven't thought about it," he replied.

"Did they give you a few days?"

"Not really. It was the older members of the commune that stirred up most of the trouble."

"I'll give you five bucks," said Pam.

"I'll consider that offer," said the kid, "but I ain't been sitting here long, and maybe the next person will give me ten or fifteen."

Pam smiled and rubbed the dog's ears one more time before she rose and took my hand. We walked toward the El Camino.

"I might be able to take eighteen," called the kid.

We kept walking.

"Okay, okay, fifteen," he shouted.

Pam and I climbed into my El Camino, and she scooted close to me as I fired up the engine.

The puppy barked at us. The kid shouted, "Think he likes you. Sure you don't want him?"

I smiled at Pam. "Well?"

"Please drive," she moaned.

I pulled us back onto the road and drove away. Pam pressed her face into my shoulder and cried silently.

A mile or so down the road, she whispered, "I just want a baby."

The roar of a jet coming in low on its approach to SeaTac Airport pulls me from my memories, and my eyes are wet as I put my tools away and lock up the garage.

I'm back in the house by two and sipping a beer while I watch Stanford jump all over Ohio State. I think about the black car I'd seen parked out front last night, and I wonder if I shouldn't call Eric.

Chances are he knows nothing about it, but I have the feeling he might know a little.

Would he tell me what he knows, or give me a line bull?

I'm guessing door number two because Eric's a chicken shit and I think he's more afraid of Jackknife than he is of me. I also think I'm too old for this game Eric and his pals are playing.

Someone is going to get hurt in a bad way before this is over, and I'd rather it not be me, but I feel I'm the one standing in the cross hairs.

I rise from my chair and fetch the .357 from the closet. I grab another beer while I'm up, and then I settle back into my chair and watch the game. Football is violent. I like it. If I'm the one in the cross hairs, so be it. I'm old and I have little to lose.

I'll take as many of them with me as I can. That's my bottom line.

That's the attitude I'd had when I came home from Vietnam.

It's not a good one. I'm not proud of it.

Believe me, I don't have to say or do things to pump myself up. I've seen what happens when people lose their grip on morality. I know what happens when anger becomes a weapon. I know the smell of guilt. I've felt the texture of darkness, and I know fear like an old friend.

I do not want these things to return to me.

I get the feeling they're close by.

I hope I'm wrong.

By midnight I'm drunk and sitting on the front porch with a loaded .357 and a twelve gauge shot gun. I'm waiting for the big black car.

The night is cold and it is raining. The rain makes a soft hissing sound as it falls into the trees and bushes and lawns. A dog is barking from a neighbor's yard several blocks away. A squirrel scampers along the top of the picket fence and disappears into the bushes.

I'm sipping whiskey as I wait.

I'm thinking this is the right thing to do. I need to find out who is in the car and what he wants. Need to put a stop to this. End it. Get it out of my life, and I know of only one way to do that.

Head on.

Running is not an option.

Of course I don't want to get my ass kicked, or get killed either, so I don't plan on fighting fair. If the big car shows I'm going to bust out a window and shove the barrel of my shotgun up someone's nose.

That's my plan anyway. I'll die trying if that's what it takes. In the real world there are no reset buttons. You have only one chance to take measure of your opponent before you pull the trigger.

Chances are the occupants of the big car feel the same way. Guess I'll find out when they show up.

But they don't.

By two, I'm nodding out, and I need to pee.

I go inside and use the bathroom. I lock up the house. I put the shotgun away and take the pistol up to bed with me.

I'm barely under the sheets before I'm sleeping.

Chapter Thirty-one

Sunday morning.

Sometimes I feel as though I'm doing time while I wait to join Pam.

Time. It seems to stand still for a moment or two, and then it slips through my life like shadows through an empty room. That's what happened to most of Saturday. It's a blank space in time that I'll never have back, and I don't care.

I just want to put distance between myself and the entire mess that my affair with Becky has caused. I want my life back. And as far as Faye goes, I sort of miss ignoring her over the fence, all though I miss being with her too, I think I can live with it either way.

I like Faye, but I don't care if she is upset with me.

If she is, you'd think she'd call and lay it out for me.

I wonder if she's expecting me to call her.

I also wonder about her problem with Jack. How much of it might be Faye. She is very attractive. I can see a man twelve years younger than her not hesitating to have an affair with her. I can also see her not hesitating to allow such an affair to happen. I think she did enjoy it. I also believe that she ended it for the reasons she had explained to me, but I don't know the time gap here. I've never paid much attention to when Faye is home or gone. I have no idea how long it's been since she called it off.

I know Faye, and yet I don't.

She claims Jack is calling and bothering her. That's none of my business, but I understand her concern.

I want space sometimes. I want to be alone. She is upset about that.

Where is her understanding?

Is she looking for a reason to call it off with me? I don't know, and I don't really feel I care either.

At nine I enter my detached garage and use a peanut grinder to remove the paint from my tail gate. I don't have pant that matches my truck, so I primer the sanded area and then I go inside to watch some football on TV.

I like the NFL. I don't have a favorite team. I usually pull for whoever is winning because more than likely, they are the more aggressive team. I like the violence of football. I know the fans in the stadiums do too. It's becoming a gladiator sport in the twenty-first century, and everyone loves it. It's the direction our culture is headed.

The big difference is, gladiators were slaves.

NFL players are paid handsomely.

They both sacrifice their bodies. They both do it to please the crowd.

At two in the afternoon I'm nursing my hangover with my second beer, and Faye calls. Her voice carries the coolness I'd seen in her eyes yesterday.

"I want you to know I understand, Matt. You need space. You're used to being alone. But when you get too lonesome you don't mind company. You're not ready for anything steady yet, and maybe I'm not either. I'm sorry I pushed a little too hard."

I close my eyes and rub my forehead.

She says, "Maybe we both need to see someone else."

I'm thinking if she wants to see Jack again, she should say so. I'm not going to be crushed.

"Is that what you want?" I ask.

"Not really."

I'm beginning to wonder what in hell does she want.

I'm not going to hurt her, but I'm going to be honest. "You're the best thing to happen to me since I lost Pam. I feel good about being with you, and I do not want you to feel used. You're right, I'm just not ready for anything steady. Being alone in my house is my comfort zone. That doesn't mean I don't want to be with you. It just means I haven't let go of Pam yet. I need time."

She's quiet.

I take a sip of beer and wonder if she understood any of it.

Finally she replies, "I don't know what to do about Jack. He won't leave me alone, and he refuses to have the lunch if you're with me. He's over reacting to the situation. I'm afraid he'll come over."

I wonder about her motive for a moment, and then I say, "If he comes over, what do you think he'll do?"

"I don't want him in my house. I'm not worried about what he'll do because I don't want him here to begin with."

"Have you told him that?"

"Of course."

"Okay," I rasp. "If he shows up, let me know."

She sighs and hangs up.

I watch football and drink beer the rest of the day, and part of the night. I'm taking a liking to the Sunday night game. I think it was a good idea, and I also think it is taking the thrill out of the Monday night game.

Let's face it, Monday Night Football is just not what it used to be. They moved it to ESPN for one thing, and for another Chris and the boys are boring. I also feel the program is too long, and if you are anything like me, you are already drunk by kickoff and lucky to make it to half time.

By the third quarter, the only people left watching the game are the diehard fans of either team, or people lucky enough to have a cushy job they can show up tired and hung-over for on Tuesday morning.

I'm fairly hammered by the end of the Sunday night game. I fall asleep in my chair, and I wake at midnight. I check the door locks and take my .357 from the closet. I climb the stairs and enter the guest bedroom. I stand at the window and wait.

I wait until two, and even though the dark sleek automobile does not drive by my house, I have the feeling it's there, out in the cold wet night. Parked just beyond my vision.

Watching my house.

I shiver as I turn away from the window.

I stagger down stairs and check all the door locks one more time.

I think about sneaking out the back door and taking the alley out to Fifth Street and circling around my block. I'll stuff the pistol in my belt and carry the shotgun. I picture myself in the act of performing this feat, creeping along the sidewalk, wet and cold and drunk, finding the big black car and approaching it.

I stop this line of thinking right there for two reasons.

One, I'm not even sure if the car is really out there, and two, I'm in no shape to confront its occupants if it is. Plus I don't know who they are or what they want, and so far they've done nothing but watch me.

Maybe I'm nuts, you know, hallucinating things. I gotta wonder sometimes.

I shake off my stupid drunk notion, and head on upstairs for bed.

What I'm thinking before I fall asleep is that I need to back off the alcohol a little. Clear my head. Find something to do to take my mind off this crazy shit.

Monday morning is sunny and clear. I know this is the last week of the fair. Seven more days of bad traffic and it's over. I'm hung over again. My head spins a little, and I feel dehydrated. I know I need a shower and a shave. I decide I'll wait until after I've had some coffee.

I reach the kitchen and notice it is already nine am on the wall clock over the small eating area. As I make a pot of coffee, I remember when Pam bought that clock from a vendor at the farmer's market in town. She loved the farmers market, and I loved watching her shop there. We'd go early to get the best prices, but most of the time she never bought anything. She just liked to look.

I run a glass of water from the faucet and down it. I run another one and take half of it. I swallow two aspirin and finish the second glass. Way I feel, I think my mother was right, I've got one foot on the gas pedal and one on a banana peel.

The kitchen fills with the smell of brewing coffee. I don't wait for the whole pot to finish. I grab a cup and fill it.

Someone knocks on the front door. I ignore it.

I doubt it's Faye. She'd call first.

I add condensed milk and brown sugar. I sip and return to the table.

They knock again.

I sip more coffee. I'm hoping they'll go away.

After a few moments they knock a third time.

I rise and carry my coffee into the living room. Through the little window at the top of the door I see a blond head.

I open the door to find Jackie Tate standing on my porch. She looks nice. She is wearing a navy dress suit and a light coat. She tosses her brown eyes over my rough appearance and smiles. "Good. I caught you at a bad time that gives me the upper hand."

I close the door in her face.

"I was only joking, Mister Conner. I apologize. Please allow me a few minutes of your time. I promise I won't take long."

I listen to her through the door and think about what she might be after. I decide it doesn't really matter anymore. I'm not going to read what she writes anyway.

I open the door and step out onto my front porch.

Jackie smells of the fall air and a mild perfume.

I smell of sleep and sweat and hung-over morning coffee-breath.

I close the door behind me and move to the bench.

Jackie follows me with her eyes. She is holding her brief case and a cell phone. "I had hoped we could use your living room," she says.

I sip my coffee. "I need some air."

"Where is Becky?"

"Who?"

She shakes her head. "I was sidetracked by another story, and I missed a lot of Becky's hospital stay. My boss wanted me to follow up on the cop who shot himself in the foot. Becky's mugging went to another journalist who got most of his information from the police. They only knew what Becky told them. Their investigation went nowhere." She pauses. "My sources, however, tell me you visited her, and picked her up when she was released from the hospital. You were driving that Lincoln next door, and Faye Evans was with you."

"What do you want, Jackie?"

"I want the truth about it. Start to finish."

"Becky's safe. That's all you need to know."

"I'll go next door and get her version. Is that what you want?"

"I want you to go away."

"Then talk to me."

I sigh and take another sip.

She waits.

"Why is this so important to you? Don't you have something better to do?"

"Not really. Besides, I'm interested. I want to know why you denied knowing Becky before you rescued her, and yet you take care of her. To me, that's interesting. To me there's a story here."

I look at her.

She smiles.

"I don't want to talk about it," I rasp.

"Why?"

"Because this is a free country and I have that right."

She gives me a frown.

I look down at the porch boards.

"All right. I'll respect that. But will you answer one question that bothers me about the whole thing?"

"Depends," I say.

"On?"

I give her a look that tells her I'm old and grey but not stupid.

She sighs and turns for the steps.

I remain seated and watch her go down to the sidewalk. She stops at the bottom and says to me, "Did you ever consider I might write some good things about you? You are pretty dog gone heroic. I have the feeling you would have intervened even if you hadn't known Becky beforehand."

I ask, "Makes you say that? You have no idea who I am."

"I'm a pretty good journalist. I'm a good judge of character, and I have a hunch you are clinging to some old fashioned notion from your generation. You're embarrassed of having had a relationship with a woman young enough to be your daughter, yet you stuck with her and made sure she was safe, even though the truth could be revealed along the way."

I say nothing.

"Well, how close am I?"

"Pretty close, but I'm no hero."

She nods. "Take care Matt Conner."

I hesitate, and then I ask, "What's the question?"

She tilts her head. "I have the feeling Becky has protected someone all along. Not you. Someone else. I'd like to know who it is, and why?"

"You're right," I say. "Because she loves him."

Jackie furrows her brow. "Bad person?"

I nod.

She turns and I watch her walk to her Escort and climb in. She does not give me another look as she starts the engine and drives away.

I rise and go back inside.

By noon I'm feeling better. I've taken a shower and I've shaved. I'm thinking about going out to the detached garage and checking on the tail gate to my Chevy. If the primer is dry, I think I'll put it on and drive up to a body shop and see if they can match the paint.

I do just that, and by two in the afternoon I'm back home and tinkering with the Mustang. The kid at the body shop told me it would be a couple days before he could get to it, but if I'd leave the tail gate and some money down on the cost of the paint, he'd take care of it for me.

I agreed, and he wrote up the order.

I tinker with the Mustang until four, and then I feel hungry, so I lock up the garage and start across my back yard. As I climb the steps on my porch, a train rushes by and fills the air with warm diesel fumes. I see Dick out raking leaves in his side yard. He waves at me. I wave back, and enter my house. I'm making a Cotto Salami sandwich with Swiss cheese when the phone rings.

I think it's Faye.

It isn't.

He sounds Hispanic when he says, "Mister Conner. I believe you owe me some money."

I feel the air slip from my lungs. "Who are you?" I ask.

"You can call me, Beto. That's Spanish for Robert."

"And how do you figure I owe you?"

"The package you had at your house for a while. When it was retrieved, it was a little light."

I say nothing. I'm thinking about Jackknife. I can see him pinching one of the baggies down, coming up with a plan and laughing about it.

"Are you still there?" asks Beto.

"Yea."

"You owe me two thousand dollars."

"Makes you think Jackknife didn't pinch the baggie down?"

"He's a business partner. There has to be a certain amount of trust."

"I wouldn't trust him as far as I could toss him."

Beto laughs.

"He's a drug addict."

"And you are not?"

"I'm sixty-two. I'm a retired rough neck. You saw my house. You saw the neighborhood I live in."

"A large amount of my customers live in neighborhoods just like yours. They drive trucks like yours. Own homes like yours. I sell a very popular product. Blue and White collar America love it."

"I wouldn't touch your product with a ten foot pole, buddy. You got the wrong guy."

"I don't think so."

"Maybe you don't, but you sound smart enough to know better than to trust Jackknife at his word. I returned the cooler untouched. If there was anything missing, you better look a little harder at Jackknife."

"You don't think I have? He has three friends to back up his story. How many do you have?"

I say nothing. I'm thinking I'm screwed and that I'd better get the two grand and give it to him. It will hurt a little, but I'll survive. I'll have to look at this as more punishment for my involvement with Becky. And I'm also thinking I'm going to kill Jackknife if I ever get a chance.

Beto sighs. "I'll give you until tomorrow evening to have the money. I'll send someone by…."

"No," I rasp. "I don't want you or your people in my home. I'll meet you somewhere up on South Hill. You name the place, and I want to see you, not some errand boy. You."

He's quiet for a moment. "Okay." He clears his throat. "The parking lot behind the theater at the mall. Know where that's at?"

"Yup."

"Eight sharp. Two grand. Don't be late and don't be light."

I hang up.

I feel like a foolish old man.

I also feel angry enough to kill Jackknife.

And I know that I have no one to blame for this mess except myself. I can't believe what I've gotten myself into. This can't be real. This can't be happening. Not to me. I'm too old for this shit.

I'm pacing the floor and thinking seriously about visiting my brother in Portland Oregon. I can simply disappear. No way would they know where I'm at. I can be gone in less than an hour.

Poof, like that.

What would Beto do? Trash my home, so what, I don't care...

Yes I do. I care a lot, and I have to do whatever it takes to prevent that from happening again. Once was enough.

I can't run from this.

I have to stand up to it.

The money is going to hurt, but I'll make it.

I only hope I stop being punished pretty damn soon.

I'm up at midnight.

I'm standing at the window looking down at the street. I have my .357 in my hand, and a small whiskey buzz in my head.

The street appears to be empty, but I don't think it is.

I turned off all the lights at ten. I sat in my chair and drank Wild Turkey, and now I'm playing a hunch. I'm thinking I need to know just how smart Mister Beto is before I face him. If he is as smart as he sounds, he will have someone watching to see if I run.

If I'm as smart as I think I am, I will find that someone just out of the butter colored glow of the street light. That someone will wait a couple of hours after I've turned off my lights, and then he'll make his phone call.

I wait. I have nothing better to do.

Fifteen minutes later, the big black car with tinted windows glides slowly through the pale street light. It stops just beyond it. A door opens and closes, and the big car moves on.

Best I can figure, the watcher was in the same bushes I'd hidden in the other night. The ones between my house and Dick's. Good choice.

Now for the other question.

I turn and walk into my bedroom with the windows facing the gravel alley out back. I unlatch the slide, and lift it about ten inches. I place my head in the cold damp air and listen. The watcher is nearly to the end of the alley before I hear the crunch of his hurried steps. I hear a car door open and then close.

I shut the window and latch it.

I lie down on my bed and close my eyes. I know Mister Beto is every bit as smart as he sounds, and that I'd better have my stitches tight when I meet him.

My last thoughts of the day are about how I might be in a world of shit right now, but at least I'm not nuts, and then I fall asleep.

Chapter Thirty-two

Tuesday is rainy.

Autumn calls at eight-thirty. I'm having coffee and toast.

"Matt," she says. "I can't make our lunch date tomorrow. Something's come up. Let's shoot for the fair Friday night. It's the last weekend of it. Have you been yet?"

"No, I haven't. Was thinking of skipping it this year."

"Oh. Well I'm sorry to cancel lunch. I was looking forward to it."

"I was too," I lie. I'd actually forgotten all about it. "But things happen," I add. "I understand."

She's quiet a moment. Then she says, "Will you think about going to the fair on Friday?"

"I will."

"Promise?"

"Yup."

"Call and let me know, okay."

"Sure."

We say goodbye and hang up. I think I'd like to get to know Autumn, but I'm not tore up about waiting. I also feel I need to tell Autumn that I'm seeing Faye, sort of, and until our relationship ends, which could happen real soon, I don't think I should date her. I sit and listen to the steady tapping of rain on the roof and I think about Faye. I really need to call her.

I stare at the phone and plan what I'm going to say, but twenty minutes later I'm still planning and staring, so I let it go for now.

I move my thoughts to Becky. I hope she is doing okay with her Aunt. I'd thought she might call me once in a while. Maybe to complain about the way things are going, or maybe to thank me because things are looking better.

Maybe she's too angry to call me.

Maybe she's too busy praying and straightening out her life.

I don't know. I still feel I did the right thing. And I also feel I'm still being punished for my affair with her.

Which brings my thoughts to the latest problem.

Beto.

I'm not completely sure what I'm going to do about him. I need a plan. I need an edge. I shower and shave while I think. I dress for the day and go back down stairs.

My chest is full of dark heavy air when I take down the .357 from the coat closet and stuff it into a pocket of my jacket. I lock up my house and leave.

I dive my Chevy to the bank and withdraw two grand from my savings account. Once the money's in my wallet, I start having doubts about how this is going to work out. Beto is obviously some sort of kingpin in the drug world. If he finds it easy to take some of my money, what's to stop him from taking more? The mindset is there.

Easy money is just that.

I need to make sure he knows the score with me, make it where it ain't so easy to take my money. Give him some second thoughts.

I need a plan that will give me an edge.

So I start to drive, and I drive all the way up Hood Canal to Port Townsend. It's a nice drive in the rain. Hood Canal is an arm of Puget Sound. It has a tide. It has beaches where people dig clams and pick oysters. In places the trees and brush grow close to the water. Creeks and small streams dump into the canal. Years ago it was a country drive. Very little traffic and most of the buildings along the water front were weekend cabins. Now, traffic is constant and beautiful homes stand everywhere. It's as though you never truly leave town.

My drive to Port Townsend takes me twice as long as it used to, but I'm in no hurry. I have all day.

I think about Pam, and I remember when we were looking for an old house to buy. We drove up here and viewed a couple of Victorian homes for sale. Pam fell in love with one of them, and we nearly bought it, but didn't because of the price tag. We had the down payment, but the monthly bill was too high, and Pam wouldn't have that. She shied away from long term debt. Treated it as though it were a plague.

I feel fortunate to be reaping the rewards of her financial strategy, but I'd trade it all away to have her still with me.

We were fortunate to find the house in Puyallup. It was cheap because it needed a lot of work, but it fit in Pam's budget, and her vision, and it is worth four times what we paid for it now.

I reach Port Townsend around noon and park my truck in a pay-lot just off the main drag. I walk down to the waterfront, and eat a basket of fish and chips for lunch. It's foggy out on the bay. The air feels wet and cool. It smells of seawater and the barnacles that cling to the old dock pilings.

When I'm finished eating, I take a walk along the wharfs. Port Townsend had at one time wanted to be a major seaport, but the railroad screwed that up when it laid its tracks to Tacoma.

I sometimes wonder about the politics in things like that. Politics have been around for a long time. Politics played major roles in both wars fought on America soil. Politics screwed the Indians and the immigrants. It's always been woven into the fabric of America, but it has never been necessary, and it played no part in making us strong.

We had politics in the Army. I also saw it at play when I was building bridges in Tacoma and drilling for oil in Alaska.

I've never had any use for it. I put it on the same shelf as I do assholes. They've been around for ever too, but we've never needed them. Matter of fact, I think the two go hand in hand.

The people who play at politics are assholes and the world would be a better place without them.

I'm good and damp by the time I return to my truck. I fire up the engine and turn on the heat. It is nearly two in the afternoon. Time to head back and come up with a plan for dealing with Beto.

I hit a liquor store in town. I buy a pint of Wild turkey 101. I leave it in the small brown bag and head back down the canal. I open the bottle when I'm a couple miles out on the road.

I know that I should not drink and drive.

I know it's not right.

But I also know it is what I need to do right now, and right or wrong I'm going to do it.

When Pam and I were first married, I had a few problems. There wasn't a lot of help for PTSD at the time, I'm glad to see there is now, but in my day there just wasn't. One of my ways to deal with my guilt and anger, was to go for a long ride and drink whiskey.

I don't remember getting drunk, but I'm sure there were many times when I shouldn't have been out driving in the condition I was in.

Pam would worry herself sick about me, and I would feel bad about what I'd done, until the next time I needed to get away, and then I'd do it again.

It's been a lot of years since I've done this. I don't remember exactly how Pam had fixed the problem. She was persistent. She was special and she loved me enough to swim through a pond full of pig shit and fetch me back if that's what it took.

I shake my head at the memories of her.

My eyes are wet and I'm struck by a memory of Pam holding on to me while the echoes of gunshots and mortars pop in my ears.

Vietnam was a bad place. I spent a year and three days over there. I caught the tail end of it, meaning, we'd already lost. It was a matter of survival at that point. We were pulling out, and the gooks wanted to kill as many of us as they could. I didn't even know what we were trying to accomplish anymore. Our government had thrown in the towel, but we were still getting shot at. American boys were still dying. I think the gooks were doing their victory dance in the end zone or something.

What a messed up place.

No wonder I came home with a bad attitude, and received an early-out discharge. My war record was perfect, but I couldn't handle the Army I went home to, and they didn't want to deal with people like me anyway.

I think America had her tail between her legs at that time.

I don't think it was so much a matter of the country being ashamed of us, but of the country being ashamed of what they'd done to us.

That's what I think, but who cares.

By seven I'm in the parking lot out back of the theater in South Hill Mall. I parked my truck around front I have the two grand waded up in the right front pocket of my jeans. In one pocket of my Carhart, I still have the .357, and in the other I have the yoyo I'd bought from the toy store in the mall. It's a cheap one, made of plastic. I have the string knotted around my index finger. I had to practice several times to make sure I can still toss one. I can. It's just like riding a bike, some things always come back to you, smooth and easy.

I feel high on whiskey.

I also feel mean and uncaring.

I have nothing to lose but my life, and it isn't worth much right now.

I've been at the mall since four. I've walked every inch of the parking lot behind the theater. I have a plan. It either works or it don't. Mood I'm in makes me think there's not a whole lot of difference between the two.

Maybe there isn't.

I'm alone in the dark. It's fairly quiet back here at this hour. I like it. I pass time by going over my plan and carrying it out in my head.

By eight I'm ready.

Beto is prompt. His black Crown Vic glides along the parking lot at eight-oh-two. I knew why he'd picked this spot the moment I'd looked it over.

This part of the parking lot is narrow. It is more of a drive through area for people wanting to exit the mall without fighting traffic. There are parking spaces to the open side of it, and the theater sits tight to the other side. It would be easy to corner someone here. Where are they going to go?

I think Beto is arrogant but cautious. I cannot see into the car, but I figure he has two in front, and one in back with him. I also know he has back up.

They had arrived about fifteen minutes ago. They did not see me because I'm tucked into the deep heavy shadows of the theater and a trash bin. They are parked about half way along the back spaces. I figure they called Beto and told him my truck isn't here yet.

He is looking now.

He is also probably holding his cell phone to his ear and listening to my phone ring.

I wait.

Beto's car eases down the lot and stops right behind the backup car.

That's a smart move.

All six of them are right there. If a threat is made on Beto's life, you would have to wade through the muscle to get to him.

I do not want to hurt him, just scare him off.

I want him to know that I didn't pinch his product, but that I'm going to pay him anyway. I also want him to know that this is the end of it. To accomplish this, I need to look him in the eyes and let him see who he is dealing with.

I wait.

I'm patient.

I learned how to be so in Vietnam. The eager die. So do the ones who rush in and try to be a hero. I'm not a hero. I'm patient. I wait for the right moment, and two minutes later, it sits right in front of me.

The Crown Vic moves past the backup car and allows it to pull out and drive off. Probably going to look for my truck out front. I watch the car disappear around the corner at the end of the lot, and I figure I have ten minutes to make my move.

Beto's car is four feet away, with the passenger side facing me.

I step from the shadows and reveal myself.

The front passenger door opens and a tall lean figure crawls out. He is dark and well groomed. His face is narrow and his eyes are black. He is wearing a suit, and he has a gun in a shoulder holster. He looks at me and says in broken English. "Stop right there."

I keep coming, closing the gap.

He reaches for his weapon, but I slip the yoyo from my pocket and let it fly. It smacks him right between the eyes. The blow doesn't knock him out, but it stuns him long enough for me to move in and finish him with a kick to the ribs. He doubles up. I grab a handful of his hair and slam his face into the roof of the car twice.

Thunk, thunk, like that.

His pistol clatters on the pavement.

He crumples and slumps against the car. I jump into his seat, and slam the door shut. I do two things that puts me in control. I jerk the .357 from my pocket and whack the driver on the side of the head. He groans as he leans into his window. I draw the hammer back for effect and point the barrel at Beto's face.

I'm surprised to see he has no one in the back seat with him.

I'm also surprised to see that he has a small pistol pointed at me.

We stare at each other. I see a short, pudgy Hispanic gentleman with long black hair combed nice and neat. He is wearing a three piece suit. He has dark eyes and a small mustache. He smells of Ax cologne.

He sees a scarred old man in wet clothing, with a mop of damp grey hair and brown eyes that are full of distance. I smell of whiskey and rain.

I lower my gun.

Beto lowers his.

The driver moans and reaches for me.

Beto growls something to him in Spanish. He stops with his fingers touching my throat. He glares at me before he turns and climbs out and closes the door. He is big, and not much of him is fat. I'm thinking I was lucky the first time, I would not want to try hitting him again.

Beto smiles.

I scratch my chin.

"Okay," he says. "What is it you wish to see me about?"

"I wanted you to get a good look at me. You can tell I'm no druggy. I also want you to know that I'm going to pay you the two grand, but that I never want to see or talk to you again."

"It's over when I say it is," he snarls.

"Then fuck the two grand."

He scowls at me, but I can see the tumblers falling in the darkness behind his eyes. "You have it on you?" he asks.

I nod.

"Why pay me if you don't feel you owe me?"

"Because I want you to go away."

He nods and says, "You really think Jackknife's friends would lie for him?"

I shrug. "I know I sure as hell didn't take any of the dope."

He digs out a cigarette, lights it, and blows the smoke toward the roof liner. He gazes out the window for a moment, and then he says, "Give me the money and we're good. If what you say is true, square it with Jackknife yourself."

"Long as it's over," I say.

He looks at me and nods. "You have my word."

"No more people watching my house," I snarl.

Surprise slips though his eyes, and then he nods again.

I dig the money from my jean pocket and hand it to him. He flattens it out and counts it. "Okay," he says.

I swing away and reach for the door handle.

"Old man," he calls.

I turn back to him.

"You got balls and you're tough, but that ain't why I'm going to let you live."

I stare at him and say nothing.

"I see in your eyes you don't give a fuck," he says while he toys with his mustache. "People that don't want to die are easy. People that don't care one way or the other are dangerous."

I nod and unlatch the door. I climb out and find that the driver has come around and helped the tall one to his feet. They are leaning against the fender. They glare at me as I walk away.

It's nine fifteen when I park my truck in its space out by the curb. I climb out and stretch. I make my way to my front porch and enter my home.

My head feels as light as a cotton ball.

The phone is ringing.

I answer it, and Faye shouts, "Matt, he's coming."

I try to remember who that might be.

"Matt," she moans. "Jack is coming over. I think he's been drinking, and I do not want to talk to him."

I scratch my forehead. I'm not sure I want to help her. I'm also not sure she even needs help. The guy used to be her lover. He's more than likely not going to hurt her.

"What are you afraid of?" I ask.

"It ended ugly," she says.

"I know that. He bruised your arms."

"Matt, please. I'm begging you to help."

I think about it for a moment. I glance at my watch.

Faye starts crying.

I'm tired. I need to pee and go to bed.

He shows up at nine-thirty. He drives a grey Lexus. He is wearing a suit and he has removed his tie. He is tall and handsome. He looks to be in good shape.

I step down off my front porch. I move across the side yard and slip through Faye's rose bushes. He's half way to Faye's porch when I intercept him. "Hey," I call. "Faye has asked me to tell you she doesn't want to see you tonight."

He stops and puts his hands on his hips. "Who are you?"

"A neighbor. We're friends."

He looks me over and smirks. "Oh, that's right, the hero. She told me about you." He pauses and staggers a little. "Why don't you crawl back under your porch and mind your own business."

"Why don't you get back in your car and disappear," I reply.

"I want to talk to her, that's all."

"Fine by me, but obviously she don't wanna talk to you."

He looks me over again.

I spread my legs a little. I'm thinking he works out in a gym. I'm thinking he is used to getting his way with people. I'm also thinking he could probably take me in a fair fight, but he has been drinking, and I don't fight fair.

He says, "How about this, pal. If you don't get out of my way, I'm going to break one of your arms off and ram it up your ass."

I shrug.

He tries to shove me out of his way, and I put him down on the sidewalk. It is easy. He has all his weight behind his move, which puts him off balance. I'm not that fast anymore, but he misjudges me. I shift to his dormant arm, and when his shove grazes my shoulder, I swung him around and down.

He is on his back in front of me. His legs are spread and his arms are out where he put them to try and break his fall. I could put a boot to his balls, and end this right now, but I don't. Instead I move over and stomp on his right hand with the heel of my shoe.

He cries out and rolls away.

I follow him.

He rolls across Faye's lawn. I kick him in the ass, and then the stomach. He yelps and moans. I stay on him and when he stops, I pin his head under my right foot.

Faye suddenly rushes out onto her porch and screams, "Stop, Matt. Stop it. You're going to hurt him."

I glance up at her. She is wearing a blue evening gown. She is holding her hands to her cheeks and crying.

I remove my foot from Jack's head and walk over to the front porch.

Faye stares at me through a mask of horror. Her mascara is running down her face with her tears. She shakes her head and holds her hands over her mouth.

I hold her eyes for a moment, and then I turn for home.

I'm wound up. I drink a beer and then another. It takes three of them to make me feel sleepy again.

When I finally lie down, I feel bad about what I did to Jack. I should have put a boot to his balls and ended it quickly.

I think about the look in Faye's eyes, and I wonder about her.

Chapter Thirty-three

C lark calls me at nine the next morning.

He says, "What are you doing old man?"

"Drinking coffee and pissing whiskey," I reply.

He chuckles.

"What are you doing?" I ask.

"Getting dressed to go to a funeral."

"Anybody I know?"

"Naw. My wife's cousin. They were close."

"No lunch today, I take it."

"Yea, hope that's okay. I talked to Steve and he wants to meet up tomorrow, if you can make it."

"I think I can."

"Good," he says. "Same place and same time."

"Yup."

We hang up and I think about Clark and Steve for a moment. I've had a lot of friends in my life. Friends in high school, and the Army. I had friends when I was building bridges and friends when I was rough necking.

I have no idea what happened to them.

We lost touch. That's life. People move on and lose touch.

Clark and Steve have been friends of mine for several years now. But it's a different type of friendship than the ones in my past. It's more of a distant relative type relationship. We care, and yet we keep our distance.

Clark and Steve came to Pam's funeral.

I would imagine they'll come to mine, or I'll go to theirs.

And that's good enough for me, because isn't that what real friends are for.

By ten, I'm out in my garage tinkering with the Mustang. I'm listening to the radio. They are playing "Heartbeat City" by The Cars and I'm remembering the time Pam bought that album for me at Christmas. It was a cassette wrapped in a huge box so I wouldn't have any idea of its contents.

She liked to trip me up when it came to gifts. She put a wallet in a shoe box one time, and on another occasion she hid a gold watch in the box her slow cooker came in.

Pam was like that. She was always throwing me a curve when I was looking for the fastball.

And I remember how busy she was around the house. She always had something to do. She busied herself right after breakfast, and didn't stop until dinner was cooked.

I couldn't tell you what she was doing half the time. I never gave it much thought. Long as she was near me, I was happy.

I'm in the house eating a honey-ham sandwich by noon. I'm having chips on the side and a glass of cold milk.

I know it is over between Faye and me. No surprise. I'd always felt it was a short term arrangement anyway. Even when Faye and I were together and happy, there always seemed to be a domino about to fall.

The way I see it, everything was true. Faye and I liked each other and we used each other. Neither of us wanted anything permanent out of our relationship. That stunt she pulled Saturday morning was her way of justifying it. She knew what she was doing when she pushed the envelope.

I see that now, and I also see how Jack played into it.

Probably about the time Faye and I started sleeping together he started calling her. As I've said before, I think she still loves him, but since he won't give in to her demands, she decided to make it rough on him.

He had to win her back, and I'll guarantee you Faye wasn't wearing an evening gown last night to take out the garbage.

Turns out Faye didn't really know a lot about me, but she knew enough to play me like a banjo.

I'm saddened by it all, yet I feel somehow relieved. I know I'm going to miss her, but I also know I'll get over it.

I'm not hurt.

With that out of the way, I move my thoughts to Eric and his pals, and I give special thought to Jackknife. The two grand he cost me didn't break me, but it hurts. It hurts because it was un-called-for and ridiculous. If I'm going to piss away my money, it will be on worthwhile things, not someone's drug habit.

I also have a feeling he's not finished messing with me. He's dinged me twice, and it was easy. To easy. He's paying no heed to the nick on his neck. That was a warning he has chosen to ignore. I have very little doubt he'll come again. His twisted line of thinking will prevail over common sense. He may be scheming something up this very moment. I don't know. I just need to stop him.

I need to call him out. I need to face him on my terms, not his.

This is something I'm not looking forward to, but it is something I feel is inevitable.

I finish my lunch and drive my truck up to the body shop. The kid has my tailgate ready. It looks pretty good. He helps me put it on and I pay him the other half of the bill. When I return home, I fetch the mail and write out a check for the utility bill, I put it in an envelope and set it on the kitchen table. I'll stick it in the box tomorrow morning. After that, I wander out to the detached garage and tinker with the Mustang for a few hours.

It is dark before I return to the house and plop down to watch some news on TV. I'm drinking my first beer when the phone rings. I have no idea who it is because I do not have caller ID. It's times like this when I wish I did.

I decide not answer it.

If it's important they will call back. They will have to because I don't have a message service either. Not on the land line.

My cell phone has caller ID and a message service, but it is back in the desk drawer with a dead battery.

Good place for it.

I'm tired, I need to pee and take a nap, and that's just what I do.

I wake at mid-night, and it is raining. I climb the stairs and enter the guest bedroom. I stand at the window and stare out at the dark, wet and empty street. I watch the rain fall through the glow of the street light. I hear it tap dance on the roof.

I suddenly feel a cold chill.

I wonder if I need to turn up the heat a little more.

I head downstairs and adjust the thermostat. I check all the door locks and slowly make my way up to my room. I strip to my boxers and crawl in bed.

I lie awake for a while. I hear the furnace come on, and I feel wafts of warm air. I think about Pam and fall asleep.

Chapter Thirty-four

It is still raining Thursday afternoon when we meet up for lunch. We are drinking beer and eating club sandwiches.

I'd had a lousy morning. I woke up depressed and spiked my coffee with 101. That's not something I would recommend for depression. It didn't help. It made me feel detached, but it didn't fill the void Pam has left in my life.

I mailed the utility bill and I watched Fox News. I started a load of laundry but forgot to move it to the drier before I left.

Steve is telling us how our country is dying from the inside out. "Values have changed," he says. "Everybody is into special interests. Everybody wants a handout. Nobody works anymore. You ever notice it don't matter what time day or night you go to Walmart, Fred Myer or even Safeway, the place is full of able bodied men walking around looking for the Cheetos. Why ain't they working?"

Clark shrugs.

I swallow a bite of my sandwich and chase it with beer. I have sort of noticed that myself, but I've really never gave much thought to it.

Steve drinks some beer and continues with, "We can't take another four years of this president."

"Why?" asks Clark.

"Because his policies are killing us."

Clark says, "But things weren't so good under George bush either."

Steve sneers, "Bullshit. Things were just fine under Bush, until the Democrats took over the congress and the senate. They made a mess of things on purpose. It was all a plan to get a liberal in the oval office."

Clark says, "You sure about that?"

Steve shakes his head and looks at me. "What do you think?"

I say, "That might be true, but it doesn't matter now."

"Why do you say it doesn't matter?"

I shrug. "We can't do anything about it."

I think Steve is going to pop a cork. His entire head turns red, and he works his mouth to say something, but it won't come out.

I'm thinking what difference does any of it make. The people in this country will vote for whomever they feel will do the most for them, just as they always have. There seems to be real hatred toward rich corporate America now-a-days, but I've made a good living off of rich corporations for all my working life. I've never wanted what the rich have because in my opinion the more you have, the more you have to worry about. I don't care about the big divide between the rich and the poor. I'm stuck in the middle and I don't mind. I pay my taxes and the government spends it on things I don't agree with, but I don't worry about it because there is nothing I can do about it anyway.

It just seems to me that a lot of people are buying into the new ideology of what America should be. They want change. Some call the promoters of change Progressives, and some call them Socialists. Not a lot of difference the way I see it. They both have the same goals.

I think the big question every American should be asking is, "What if they're wrong?" And how about this, "What does political correctness, diversity, gay marriage, and abortion have to do with making a country strong in the first place?

Were the promoters of the sexual revolution right? The sixties brought us free love, and the seventies brought us the dysfunctional family.

I don't know.

I just don't know if we are a better and stronger country. And I don't care anymore. I'm pushing the twilight. I just want to be left alone.

But Steve looks as though he's about to have a heart attack. So Clark and I calm him down by telling him he is right.

"We need to care," says Clark. "There is something we can do about it."

"You bet," I add. "The bastards aren't going to get away with it."

Steve's color returns to normal.

He nods and thinks about it for a moment, and then he says, "Let's have another beer. Hey, you hear about how Harry Reed is sitting on all those bills passed by Congress and he won't even recognize 'em?"

Clark winks at me, and waves at our waiter.

I think it's funny how Steve wants us to agree with him that we are screwed, our country is dying, and we need to care about it, but he knows we can't do anything about it. So he just moves on to another problem.

I wonder if Steve feels he's just the messenger. I know he was a radioman in Vietnam. Maybe he's still carrying the radio.

I'm headed home by three. I'm driving down South Tacoma Way, and I'm wondering how Becky's doing when I see a jewelry store with a sign out front that reads: Cut Rate Jewelry.

I drive right by it. I'm thinking no way, but something is telling me different, so I find a place to do a U-turn, and I drive back to the store and park out front.

The gentleman behind the counter looks Middle Eastern. He is wearing a black suit and tie. His azure eyes study me as I enter and walk over to the glass case where the rings are on display.

"Something I can help you find," he says in butchered English.

"Just browsing," I say.

He watches me as I look through the glass at all the rings. Must be fifty or sixty of them, and I'd know Pam's out of a thousand if it's here, but I don't see it. I'm not sure how these places operate, but I've watched Pawn Stars and I know you can out right sell something, or take a loan against it. I figure Jackknife would sell it.

I also figure he either lied about where he hawked it, or the gentleman from the Middle East has already sold it.

"This all the rings you have?" I ask.

He nods solemnly.

"You sell very many of them?"

"Is that your business?"

I look him in the eyes and see that he is in no mood to answer questions from a grey haired old white man. It also dawns on me that this guy has no way of knowing whether he is buying stolen jewelry or not. People slide in here with a ring and some trinkets. He figures what he can give them and still make money, and the deal is done.

I turn and walk out.

I fire up my truck, but I don't drive away.

Not yet.

A notion is clawing up my back like a cat on a curtain. I look around and see any number of hawk shops and jewelry stores within a block of this place. This portion of South Tacoma Way is notorious for them, and hookers, wineos and the homeless too.

Why did Jackknife name this place?

The gentleman from the Middle East is staring at me.

I put my truck in gear and back away. I angle out to the street and look for an opening in traffic. I see one and jump into it. I'm thinking Jackknife did sell Pam's ring to the gentleman in the black suit. I'm also thinking he still has it.

The way I see it, they know each other. The man from the sand knows that Jackknife is a drug addict and a thief. Of course the ring wouldn't be on display yet. It was still cooling off. The man is no dummy. He's not going to display a freshly stolen item. Not yet. He might sell it out the back door, but he's not going to put it on display.

The owner might walk in, or in some instances, if the article is worth enough, maybe the police. I'm thinking he'll let the item cool for at least a month or longer.

Every fiber of my conscience is telling me I'm better off to let it go, yet I know in my heart that I'm not going to do that. I also know it's possible I'm all wrong about the jewelry store and how things work, but I don't think so.

I think I'm right and that this is my chance to make a move before Jackknife does. I need to put him down, toss his body in a dumpster and be done with it.

And I'd also like to have the ring back, just for personal reasons.

Chapter Thirty-five

Number one, Pam, on her deathbed, made me promise I'd bring it with me, and number two it just isn't right.

It wasn't right for them to come into my house and rob me. It wasn't right for them to involve me in their drug world to begin with. I wasn't going to stand by and watch a man beat a woman. I'd have stopped Eric from pounding on Becky, even if I hadn't known her.

There are some things in this world that we as humans must never tolerate. One of them is abuse, whether child or adult. Another is rape, and another is murder, especially the murder of the defenseless. Still another is theft. We had thieves in the Army and we had our own way of dealing with them. I'm going to deal with Jackknife in a similar fashion, and then take it a step further.

I call Eric at four. I figure he's up and getting ready for work by now.

He answers on the fourth ring.

"Low."

"Eric, Matt Conner. I need to get a hold of Jackknife."

He's quiet for a moment or two, and then he says, "Why you wanna see him, man. He's bad news."

"It's a personal matter between him and me. I just want to talk to him. Can you arrange it?"

"Don't know. I can tell him. Don't mean he'll do it."

"Try for me, will you?"

"Yea, okay."

Jackknife calls two hours later.

"You got balls, old man. I ought to come over there and break your fucking head open for you, after what you put me through. Beto won't have nothing to do with me no more, cause of you."

"I'm the one out two grand," I growl.

"Yea, and I'm on a shit list. Think I care."

I've got a smart-ass comeback for that, but I don't use it. I wait a moment, listen to him breathe into the phone. I clear my throat and say, "I think I know where the ring is, and I need your help getting it back."

He continues to breathe into the phone.

I wait him out.

"Makes you think I'd help you?"

"Money," I say.

He laughs, and I hear him light up a cigarette before he asks, "How much money?"

"Whatever the ring is worth. I'll buy it back and pay you double the price."

He thinks about that for a moment.

I add, "It's gotta be just you and me, Jackknife. Your buddies can't tag along. Just us."

He chuckles. "I don't need any help fucking you up."

I say nothing.

"You still there?" he asks.

"We got a deal or not?"

"How do you think you know where the ring is?"

I hesitate. "You told me, remember?"

He thinks about that for a moment. "Don't fuck with me, old man."

"I'm not. I'm playing a hunch."

"You don't know what you're doing."

"Sounds like a chicken-shit answer to me."

"Fuck you. Alright, man. How do you want to do this?"

"Meet me at the jewelry store, nine sharp."

He hangs up.

I know he is going to do one of two things. He's going to call the gentleman from sand land, or go see him. I'm not sure what kind of relationship they have, probably all business. I figure he'll refuse at first, but eventually they'll settle on a price. I figure the price will be way high, and Jackknife thinks he's going to win on both ends of the deal. He also thinks he's going to stamp my envelope, and walk away with the ring and the money when it's over.

And that's okay with me.

It's simply all the more reason to do what I have in mind.

Faye calls at eight.

I hear a lot of casino noise in the back ground.

"Matt," she says. "I'm at Ocean Shores, staying at the casino."

I say nothing.

"You scared me the other night. I didn't know. I thought. I feel I should thank you, but...."

"That's okay," I sigh.

She's quiet

I'm quiet.

"Matt. You still there."

"Yes."

"I'm with Jack," she blurts.

I shrug.

She says. "He's going to divorce his wife."

"Oh yea."

"I don't want you to feel I used you, hope you don't, and I'm still not sure about all this just yet."

"Are you happy?"

"I think so, yes."

I'm thinking she is, but not as much as she'd thought. I scratch the whiskers on my chin and say, "I gotta run Faye. Maybe we'll talk when you get back."

"I'd like that, yes."

We hang up. I wonder what she is up to, but I decide not to give it a lot of thought. Not now, maybe later, or maybe never.

I go upstairs and dig through my sock drawer until I find the one I want. It's a nice heavy wool one. I set it down and move to the closet. I dig around until I find the piggy bank. It's an old one, the kind you have to break to get the money. It is full of pennies.

The burglars had missed it, but they probably would have broken it open and left it if they'd have found it anyway.

A penny doesn't buy much now-a-days, even a handful of them doesn't amount to much.

The bank was made of ceramic. Pam had bought it at the Farmer's Market. She'd bought it from a woman who made all sorts of cute little things. I remember how Pam and the woman had hit it off, and talked for an hour before we bought the piggy and moved on.

I remember Pam telling me she was going to fill it with pennies and save them for a rainy day.

The rainy day has arrived I think as I smash the ceramic piggy on the floor.

Chapter Thirty-six

I'm up at five. I'm drinking coffee and feeling like a foolish old man who is about to get his ass stomped on royally.

I can't help it.

I'm thinking I need to let it go.

As I've said before, I can apologize to Pam and she'll understand. I've never been much on principles. I was a kid when I went to Vietnam, and I came home angry as hell. I was mean and calloused, until I met Pam.

But she's gone.

As I stare at the whiskey bottle in front of me, I feel mean again. I feel angry and full of sin.

I lift the bottle and take a sip.

I feel the burn all the way down.

It's only a matter of time before Jackknife wants more from me. He'll keep coming and taking until there's nothing left. It's a game to people like him. It's a way to feed his hunger too, but mostly it's a game because what he hungers for is only a part of it.

His brain is fried. He is twisted and evil.

I'm going to kill him.

I drive into South Tacoma, and park my truck in a busy park-and-ride lot located two blocks from the jewelry store. It is six-thirty when I climb out and lock the door. I'm wearing the Carhart jacket and I have the sock, a quarter full of pennies, in my pocket. I feel reckless, but cautious too.

In a situation like this, you can be overly cautious, or far too reckless. You can get killed by either one. You can also use both of them at the right level to motivate you. I'm not going to take chances, but I'm not going to hesitate either. My gut feeling will guide me.

It stopped raining sometime last night. Clouds are scattered across the sky and the wind is blowing. The air feels chilly and smells of traffic and wet asphalt.

I make a wide circle around the building. It has no alley. The back door gives way to a small parking lot. Some dumpsters are lined up along a side street, and the side street is lined with other small businesses. I see a few homeless people digging through the dumpsters. I see a couple of hookers who look to be waiting for their pimp to come pick them up. I tighten my circle and get a good feel of the place, and then I walk back to my truck and drink whiskey and wait.

Eight o-clock I drive to the side street and park in front of a small coin shop. It's not open yet. I sit and watch the back door of the jewelry store. The gentleman from the Middle East shows up at eight-thirty, and Jackknife shows up five minutes later. They both park in back. The owner of the store drives a Lexus. Jackknife is in the Dodge clunker.

I wait ten minutes before I climb out and approach the back door. I figure it's locked, and I'm right. I walk back to my truck and wait until nine straight up before I drive around front. I'm glad the back door is locked from the inside. That way there will not be any surprises.

The closed sign is still hanging in the window.

I park my Chevy and climb out. I stuff my hands into the pockets of my jacket and move to the front door. I knock and wait.

Jackknife opens it, and I can tell right away that he is flying high on his speed. The dark gentleman is standing in the very same spot he stood yesterday.

I nod at him, and he nods back.

Jackknife says, "You think you're pretty smart, don't you?"

I say nothing.

Jackknife closes the door and locks it. He gives me a shove toward the sales counter. I half turn to him.

"Don't act like you ain't scared, fucker," he growls.

"Where's the ring?" I ask.

"How much money'd you bring?" he replies.

"What I thought," I say as I pull the sock from my pocket.

The dark man shuffles his feet. He's eyes flutter. He wants no part of this. It was supposed to be easy. No rough stuff until afterwards.

Jackknife glares at me. "You ain't doing shit, old man."

I hit him with the sock, right in the center of his forehead.

"Fuck," he growls and stumbles away. I stay right on him. I hit him again behind the ear. He moans. I know he's seeing stars and hearing train whistles. I reach around him and remove his pistol. It's a .38. Nice and light and deadly. I toss it over the glass counter and it hit's the floor with a thud.

"The ring," I say as I turn to the sales counter.

The dark man has it in his hand. He stares at me and hesitates, and then he sets it down and slides it toward me. I pick it up and drop it into my pocket.

"How much did you give for it?" I ask.

"One-fifty," he says.

I remove my wallet and pay him.

He looks surprised. He backs away and stares at the money on the counter in front of him.

Jackknife is recovering. His ear is bleeding, and he has a knot on his forehead. He gives me a fuzzy "You're dead" look.

"Back door," I say.

He staggers around the glass counter. I know the stars are falling and the whistle is a whisper now.

The gentleman from the Middle East walks to the door and opens it. He steps aside.

Jackknife walks out first.

I see him reaching into his coat pocket. I figure it's a knife. The nickname. It's not rocket science.

I follow him out.

The dark man closes the door behind me. Jackknife walks to his car and turns as he leans against the fender. He shows me the knife. It's not a switch blade, but it's long and deadly.

"Stupid old man," he growls.

I stare at him.

He swings the blade around in the air. The way he holds the knife, I can tell he knows how to use it.

"I'm going to cut your fucking throat," he snarls.

I nod. I'm holding the sock of pennies down at my side.

He looks at it. He's already had a taste of it. He knows how much it hurts, and he wants to take me without being hit again.

I watch his eyes. I see the tumblers falling into place. He is planning how to do this. He is not stupid. He has the advantage. He's flying high on his speed.

"I'm going to kill you, Jackknife," I say. "You're a piece of shit, and I'm going to beat you to death."

"You're the one going to fucking die," he sneers.

I shrug.

He looks into my eyes. The tumblers move again. He sees the truth standing right in front of him. A calloused old man who does not care anymore.

A police car suddenly stops out on the side street. The officer inside takes a good long look at us before he slowly moves forward.

Jackknife quickly puts the blade away while he shakes his head at me.

"This ain't over," he snarls and climbs into his Dodge.

I stuff the sock into my coat pocket and head for my truck. I reach it, and as I'm about to climb in, the police car pulls up behind me, and the officer rolls down his window.

I turn to him.

He looks to be in his forties. He looks tired and serious. "People hang out in this area for one of two reasons," he rasps. "They are buying drugs, or they are buying a blow job."

"Don't need either," I say.

"Where'd your pal go?"

"You scared him off."

I can see in his brown eyes that he appreciates me not playing any games with my answers. He yawns and says, "I broke something up, right?"

I nod.

He cracks a smile and drives off.

Chapter Thirty-seven

I'm not as wound up as I'd thought I'd be. The thing with Jackknife is no big deal.

Could I have killed him?

Absolutely.

I know I would have beat him to death, but I'm glad I didn't. Killing is not something I want to do again. I will if I have to, but I'm not looking forward to it. Most people, especially younger ones, have their heads to far into what Hollywood and video games have depicted as killing. Believe me, ask any veteran who has seen real action, killing is a serious matter. Whether it is done out of fear, anger, or self-defense, it is forever a reality in your conscience.

I think Clint Eastwood defined it best in the movie "The Unforgiven." He said that it was a hell of thing to do. I'm not sure of his exact words, but he goes on to say something about how when you kill a man, you take away everything he had, has or ever will have.

Don't think I'm concerned about Jackknife's past, present and future, but I am concerned about mine.

When I came home from Vietnam, it took me ten years to put the nightmares down. Pam helped me because she loved me, and she was a special person.

Whiskey helped too. It was my anodyne until I realized I had to make a choice between it and Pam. I chose Pam, but she's gone now.

I'm all alone, and the doorway back to what I was is wide open.

Jackknife isn't worth it.

I think about Faye and realize how much I used her. I used her to maintain a sense of balance in my life. She represented normality in the chaos that was caused by my affair with Becky.

Turns out she was up to her own little game and used me as well, but I still feel I need to talk to her about us. I'd like to clear the air and maybe start over, but I don't think that is in her plans.

I reach home by nine-thirty.

I know I'm supposed to have a date tonight with Autumn, but I'm thinking of excuses as I make coffee and watch the morning news on TV.

By noon I'm working on the Mustang that I do not plan to ever finish. I listen to classic rock music and I think about Pam while I tinker with the throttle linkage.

I remember the time we made love in this car. It was shortly after we'd bought it and had it towed home. I was pulling the engine with a four-way strap and a chain fall I'd fastened to a beefed up ceiling beam. It was in August and it was hot. I'd removed my shirt and used it to wipe the sweat from my forehead.

Pam brought me a glass of ice tea and a tuna fish sandwich around noon. She was wearing a pair of jean shorts and a tank top t-shirt. It was a period in her life when she had trouble keeping weight off. I thought the extra weight looked nice on her. It filled out her butt cheeks a little, that's all. But she was always conscious of it.

I pinched a butt cheek when she leaned over to set the tea and sandwich down on my tool box.

She turned and tossed me a cloudy eyed look, and next thing you know, we were trying to knock a hole in the seats.

I suddenly think I smell her presence in the garage and my eyes get misty. I remember how that simple task of making love to her made her feel better about herself, and how I never wanted more than what we had together.

I'm back in the house by two. I realize I haven't eaten anything all day, so I decide to make a tuna fish sandwich. Mine doesn't taste as good as Pam's did, but they are eatable. I have some chips and a pickle on the side. I pour a glass of milk and sit at the table. I think about Pam's wedding ring while I eat. I'm not taking any more chances with it. From now on I'll carry it with me where ever I go. That way I'll always have it.

With that decided, I finish my sandwich and move to the living room. I plop into my chair and use the remote to turn on the TV. I set the volume low. I'm suddenly very tired. I guess my activities have caught up to me. It was a short night and a long morning. I'm sleeping within minutes.

I wake at four to a ringing telephone.

I'm drowsy when I answer it.

"Matt, did I wake you?" asks Silva.

"No problem, I need to get up anyway."

"You okay?"

"Yea, I'm good. I'm retired, Silva. I can take a nap whenever I feel like it."

She laughs.

I wait.

"How's it going with Autumn, do you like her?"

"I haven't had much of a chance to get to know her yet."

"That's too bad. I hope you give it a try. I think you'll like her."

I shrug. I'm thinking Autumn has called her and told her about the cancelled lunch, and she's thinking I might be hesitant now, and maybe Silva can shore up her chance at another date."

She says, "I worry about you Matt. It's not good for you to be alone so much. You still seeing Faye?"

"Naw. We sort of called if off for a while."

"No loss there, believe me."

I wonder what happened between her and Faye, but I don't ask.

Silva says, "Call Autumn. I think she is more your type."

I wonder what she means by that, but I don't ask.

"Well, anyway, I gotta run. Promise me you'll call Autumn."

I hesitate.

"Matt?"

"Ok, I'll call her."

She makes a noise that I envision goes with a victory pump.

I open my wallet and remove a business card. It has Autumn's job title and phone number on it. I know that if

I don't call her, it's over and I will never know what she is really like. I also know that if I date her and we like each other it might end the same way it ended with Faye.

I didn't want to scare Faye, or use her, but I know I did. Now, far as I'm concerned, it was fun while it lasted.

I have to wonder how Becky was so close to being right about Faye, and Silva so far off. Or was I being paraded around a little as well. Were both of them right to a point? Guess I don't know. I'm a beat up old man who doesn't care anymore. That's all I am, and the way I feel right now, I don't need another woman in my life.

I dial Autumn's number, and she answers after three rings.

"Hello, Matt."

"How'd you know it was me?"

"Have your number in my contacts."

I have no idea what that means as I say to her, "I'm going to take a rain check tonight, something's come up."

She's quiet for a moment, and then she replies with, "Okay. Maybe some other time."

"Yea," I say. "Maybe."

"You're too old for cold feet, Matt," she blurts.

"To old for a lot of things."

She laughs.

I wait.

"You don't want to go to the fair this year?"

"No. Was thinking of passing on it."

"Any particular reason?"

"Didn't know I needed one."

"Wow. Okay. Guess that sums it up."

She hangs up.

I stare at the floor and think about the quiet around me. It doesn't seem that good anymore. I still like it, and yet I don't. Not all the time anyway, and for some reason not tonight.

I pick up the phone and dial Autumn's number again.

She lets if ring twice before she answers with, "Yes, Matt. Was there something else?"

"You said you had me listed in your contacts. What does that mean?"

"Well, it's like a phone book in your phone. You don't have to remember a bunch of phone numbers when you want to call people. You just open your contacts and find the person you wish to call, and click on them."

"Sounds handy."

"It is. I keep all my friends on there, business associates, and special numbers." She pauses. "You do have a cell, right?"

"Yea, but it's an old one."

She's quiet for a moment, and then she asks, "Was that it?"

"No. I don't feel good about the way I handled our conversation a moment ago. I'm rusty at making friends. I don't know how to do this stuff."

"Is that an apology?"

"I don't know."

She laughs.

I stare at the floor.

"Tell you what," she says. "I'll be at the blue gate at seven sharp."

She hangs up.

I'm wondering why I'm doing this as I shower and shave and dress in clean Lee jeans and a collared pull over shirt.

I think it's to put distance between myself and my dead relationship with Faye. I also think it's because I simply want to see Autumn again.

Why not?

She's attractive, and she's made more than a decent effort to have this date. Maybe I need to find out why.

It'd be nice to know what she sees in me.

It would also be nice to know what I see in her.

So what the hell.

I lock up and leave the house at six-thirty. It's about a twenty minute walk to the fair grounds. I stuff my hands into my front pockets. I smell the fair and gaze at the skyline all aglow from the lights. I can see the roller coaster and the fair's wheel. I hear the roar of people. The night air is warm and it feels thick around my face.

The last weekend is always the worst when the weather is nice. I see people from every walk of life around me, and I realize it doesn't really matter how screwed up our government is, we the people are still going to enjoy the same things our grandparents did.

The blue gate is all the way around on the Meridian side of the grounds. I make my way through the crowd, and I see Autumn before she sees me.

She looks fantastic. She is wearing black shorts and a pink sleeveless blouse. She is dolled up. Her hair is a mountain of ginger curls. Her lips are ruby red. Her breasts are pushing hard against the blouse.

I can't help but notice how her eyes light up when she sees me approaching her.

She smiles and takes my hand. "Glad you could make it," she says.

The first thing I learn about Autumn is that she loves being independent. She's already bought all the tickets we need to enter the grounds, and to enjoy several of the rides. She informs me of this as we squeeze through the gate.

"What if I didn't show?" I ask.

"Your loss," she smiles.

She leads me straight over to the roller coaster, and as we wait in line, she asks me, "Why were you dragging your feet?"

I scratch my head and shrug.

She squeezes my hand. "Come on. I want to know you."

"Not sure," I say. "Some things have happened lately that sort of took me out of my routine."

"Oh. A man of routines."

"Yea. I sort of like order. Keeps me in balance."

She nods. "I'm like that to a point. But I'll throw caution aside at times and take a chance."

"Like tonight?"

She nods. "I had a backup plan though."

I don't ask.

She tells me anyway. "I've been seeing Fred for a couple months. He's boring, but nice and predictable."

I sigh. "Is he home waiting for your call."

"No, he's here somewhere. I told him to meet me at seven fifteen."

I'm still absorbing that when we climb into our car and go for a ride. I decide not to comment on it. I decide I like Autumn already, and that I may as well see where she goes with this.

Why not?

Pam is probably laughing.

After the roller coaster, we ride the fair's wheel, and then the bumper cars before we finally take a break. I buy the hotdogs and drinks. We sit across from each other at a small plastic table.

I'm interested. I like the way she holds me with her eyes. I think she likes to tease, and I'm fine with that.

She chews on her hotdog and says, "I know about Faye. Silva filled me in on her and you and…." She pauses and takes a drink of her Coke. "Anyway, it's none of my business, and Good Lord I'm the last one to hand out advice, but you are damn handsome, Matt, and Silva was right about you. You've got the look."

"The look?"

She reaches over and touches my chin. "Yup."

I blush and recover. "What about Fred?" I ask.

"I don't love him and I use him."

"Miss Independent."

She tosses me a naughty look.

We eat in silence for a moment, and then she says, "I know a lot about you already. Silva thinks you're the one for me. So you have a lot to live up to."

I like her boldness. I want to know more, but I'm in no hurry.

She says after a big gulp of Coke, "I'm fifty-five, Matt. I want you to know that I'm looking for the right guy, but I'm going to have fun along the way. I was a mother and a housewife in my youth, and being both of them disappointed me. I'm not going to bore you with the details." She winks.

I say, "I doubt anything about you could be boring."

She laughs. "Are you glad you showed up?"

"Oh yea."

She finishes her hotdog and tosses off the remainder of her drink. She stands and reaches for my hand. "The best is yet to come."

I gather our mess and toss it into a garbage can. I rise and take her hand.

She leads me to a ride that has been around forever. It's a new version of it, but the effect is the same.

And the second thing I learn about Autumn is that she gets what she wants when she wants it.

We snuggle in the little cart, and as soon as we are alone in the dark tunnel, we start to kiss. She goes exploring with her hand before I do, and she touches the places she wants to know about. The muscles in my shoulders and arms, and then my hairy chest, and then she is down to the little roll around my belt. She pinches me there, and giggles.

I touch her breasts and her tummy, and then I grab a hand full of her butt, and she moans into my ear as she nibbles on the lobe.

We pull apart as the lights hit us, and I like the way she is blushing just a little, and the way she waits for me to help her from the cart.

Her cell phone suddenly starts vibrating. She glances at it and gasps, "Oh Matt. It's poor Fred. I'd better answer."

I step away to give her some privacy.

She talks for a few moments, and then she puts her phone away and smiles at me as she approaches.

"He's still out front. He's frantic. I'd better go."

I nod.

She puts her hands on my chest, and gives me a look that could make a glass of ice water boil. I have the feeling chapter two for us is just around the corner.

She plants a small wet kiss on my lips and turns away.
I watch her go, and like what I see.

I'm sitting in my easy chair, drinking a beer and watching an old John Wayne western. It is nearly ten.

I'm thinking about Autumn.

The phone rings and I think it might be Faye.

"Hey, old man," says Eric. "We got a problem."

"My name is Matt, and by we you must mean you and the turd in your pocket."

"Becky said you promised her you'd help me."

"You been talking to Becky?"

"Yea. We still might get back together, you know, but she won't have anything to do with me unless I'm clean."

I say nothing.

"You still there?"

"Yea. Why ain't you at work?"

"Took the night off, man. Called in sick."

I shake my head.

"They're talking about starting drug tests down at the shop, they are warning everybody to get clean, you know, so I been thinking about getting into a program and getting off this shit. Clean up. I don't want to lose my job, and I'd like to see Becky again."

"So."

"Jackknife ain't going to let that happen, man. He said he ain't done with me, and he said he still has a score to settle with you too."

"Tell Jackknife to kiss your ass."

"You know I can't do that, man."

I sigh.

Eric says, "I need your help getting out of this mess I'm in. I know you're not afraid of him. I figure maybe you could tell him to leave me alone or something."

"You think he's going to listen to me."

He says nothing.

"Where is he now?"

"I don't know. Not here right now, but he might come by later. He uses my house to stash shit because he says it's safe."

"Were you in on the pinched baggy?"

"The what?"

"A guy named Beto charged me two-grand for stealing some of his dope."

"Oh, that. Yea, Matt, I sort of was."

I think about it. I want to tell Eric he's on his own. When I promised Becky I'd help Eric I didn't mean it. I just said it to get her to go to her aunt's place. I don't want anything to do with these people. I'm to old for this shit. I want to be left alone. And I also think Eric has a lot of nerve asking me for help when he was in on Jackknife's scheme."

Eric says, "You still there."

"Yea. I really don't think there is anything I can do for you. Don't you have any friends that are clean and would be willing to help you?"

"No."

"Go to the police."

"Yea, right, man. What are they going to do? Probably throw me in jail."

"You'd be safe."

"Till I get out. I can't stay in jail until Jackknife dies or something."

"I don't need your problems Eric. I can't help you."

"He is going to fuck with you too, man. He's really pissed at you."

I rub my forehead.

"You shouldn't have slapped him around like that. You shouldn't have poked him with a tire iron, and beat on him with a sock full of shit. You can't do that with people like him and get away with it."

I shrug. "Tell me how Jackknife convinced a man as smart as Beto to go after me instead of him?

"He told Beto that you were a customer. You came over acting like you wanted to score, but had bigger intentions. You pulled a gun on me, whacked me with it, took the product and hauled ass. He told Beto that we went after you, but you weren't home, so we trashed your place and took what was left of the stuff."

"Beto bought that?"

"Not at first. I thought he was going to kill all four of us, but Jackknife can be pretty convincing, man. Told Beto there was a rat in the system and that's how you knew about the cooler. Said it could have been my ex-girlfriend, Becky. She disappeared. You should hear Jackknife when he's in a pickle. That, and he had the three of us to back up his story. We all practiced what to say, so our stories didn't conflict with each other."

"And you did your part?"

He hesitates. "Yea, man, I didn't want to die. Sorry about that."

"Well I'm sorry too, Eric," I rasp and hang up.

I finish my beer and fetch another one from the fridge. I'm half way through it when the phone rings again.

This time it's Becky.

"Matt," she says. "You gotta help Eric. He might lose his job. If he stands up to Jackknife he'll get hurt bad, or worse. Please, Matt, help him."

"You don't know the whole story, Becky."

"Know I still love Eric and want what we once had. And I do know the whole story. He told me. I'm asking you to forgive him and keep your promise."

I think about what she's just said, and I ask, "You love a man that won't stand up for himself?"

"Yes. Because I know he will stand up for himself someday."

"Not a chance," I say.

She starts crying.

I wait.

She cries for a few minutes, and then she says, "Okay, Matt Conner. Don't live up to your end of the deal. I'll forgive you." And she hangs up.

It is not as much the two grand Eric cost me, as it is the principle of the thing. That's what I'm thinking as I go back to my John Wayne western.

Five minutes later, it hits me. I have to help Eric. The principle of it doesn't matter. I made a promise. I didn't make that promise with good intentions, but I made it.

If a man cannot be taken at his word, then what's left of the man?

I pick up the phone and dial his number.

"Hello," he says.

"Ok," I growl. "If Jackknife shows up tonight, tell him to call me."

"Thanks, Matt," he says.

"And one more thing. If this is one of Jackknife's plans to get me. I will kill you for being involved. Is that clear?"

"Yea, Matt."

I hang up.

I go back to my movie. I think about Autumn again, and I remember when Pam and I used to ride into the tunnel of love. We enjoyed that ride as much after forty years of marriage as we did when we first met. I wonder about Autumn. Did it mean anything to her, or is she in the tunnel right now with Fred.

I decide I don't care.

I decide she has the ball in her court, and she likes it that way.

I have to smile, and then my smile fades as I start thinking about Eric.

The situation with Eric reminds me of no other situation I've ever faced.

I sort of like something about Eric, but I dislike way more about him. He's from the generation of sissy boys and stupid white girls. They should be called generation nowhere. They are lost. The people who wanted to destroy America used our education and entertainment systems to brainwash them. They do not have a clue what America is about. They have been told that America was all wrong, it was an experiment and it failed.

They couldn't mop the hallways of the schools I went to. They don't understand the concept of true freedom, believe me, it's not free. It never was and it never will be. Nothing is free. Someone has to suffer, or maybe even die. No one has a right to anything unless they work for it.

And the generations coming after them are even worse.

They don't even know what the truth is anymore. The truth could hit them on the side of the head, and they wouldn't recognize it. They are not even worth the effort.

Enough of this.

I don't care anymore.

Chapter Thirty-eight

Jackknife calls at mid-night.

I'm ready for him. I've thought this out, and I've decided that I'm not going to spend the rest of my life worrying about him, wondering when he might hit. I had every intention of killing him this morning, and I have every intention of finishing it tonight.

I'm sitting in my easy chair.

I'm sipping whiskey now.

Jackknife says, "No deals, old man. You are dead fucking meat. So save your breath."

"Not after a deal. Not with you," I growl.

"Then what do you want?"

"Leave Eric alone. Find somewhere else to hide your shit."

He chuckles. "Man you got balls."

I wait.

"Why you care about Eric?"

"He asked for my help. He wants to clean up. You need to move on anyway. You're dragging the whole neighborhood down."

"Oh yea, well fuck you, old man. You screwed up my deal with Beto, and now you want me to give up my safe house."

"You screwed up your deal with Beto. It cost me two grand. I would have killed you this morning if the cop hadn't showed up."

He breathes heavy into the phone.

I say nothing.

He breaks the silence with, "You got balls, and you talk the talk, but heads up you ain't no match for me. You think I'm stupid, but I'm not. I fucked the shit out of the woman 'cause she was yours, not Eric's. He's a pussy. I'm not. That cop saved your ass, not mine. Any time you want some of me, come get it."

I think about what he's said.

"Don't die on me yet," he barks.

"Let's get this over with," I growl. "Enjoy the last five minutes of your life."

"Bring it on, fuck-face."

I hang up.

I am fairly certain of two things. One, five minutes isn't enough time for them to come up with a decent plan, and two, whatever Jackknife has in mind to do to me isn't going to work because I'm going to kill him.

I've thought this through, and I've realized that my world will never be right again until Jackknife is gone. He's like a bag of monkey shit hanging in a flower shop. He doesn't fit.

He might be right about me being no match for him straight up, but he is underestimating me if he thinks I care. I'm running on whiskey and adrenaline. Are they enough? I'm not sure. I only know that I feel real mean, and when I feel that way I will do things I normally wouldn't do.

Things from my past. They bring me no good memories. Only anger.

I open the coat closet and reach way in back. The Whiffle ball bat is still there. Dick's kids left it in my yard a long time ago. When I tried to return it, he told me to keep it. He said that the kids use it to beat on each other when they are not playing Whiffle ball. I hold it up to the light. It is blue and light and easy to swing. It has just enough weight to it, to put some snap on the end when it strikes a target.

Seven minutes later I pull to the curb out front of Eric's house. I kill the engine and climb out. I stuff the bat half way up under my Carhart jacket, and check to make sure the pistol is in my right hand pocket. I walk around the bed of my truck .

Jackknife's two pals are waiting at the end of the driveway. Both of them are trying to look mean. One of them has a short piece of pipe in his hand, and the other one is opening and closing his fists.

The one with the pipe says, "Looky here, Josh. It's old man time."

I can tell right away that they are not fighters. They are just punks who have probably only beaten up people who were already done for. They let me get way to close, and they are not ready.

In one not so fast and smooth motion, I whip out the bat and pop the kid with the pipe on the end of his nose. He drops the pipe and reaches up for the broken bone, blood and tissue in the middle of his face. I lower my aim and put a ground ball smacker square into his balls. He moans and drops to his knees. I plant my foot in his chest and knock him over.

The one he'd called Josh hits me in the ear with his fist, and then he moves back toward the parked Dodge.

My ear is hurting bad enough to really piss me off as I go after him.

He tries to spin away, but I nail him one across the shoulder that stings like fire. He swings at me with his left arm, and catches my eye brow. I slump down and come around with the bat. A lot of my upper body weight is behind the swing, and I nail it hard into his midriff.

The air and the fight go out of him.

I give him some stars to see with a couple thumps on the back of his head.

I watch him go all the way down and slightly out before I turn my attention to the front door of Eric's house. I know Jackknife has a gun and a knife, but at this point it's all about the killing. I'm breathing hard and the adrenaline is pumping up bubbles in my chest.

I toss the bat out toward my truck, and grab the gun in my pocket as I move up the sidewalk. I reach the front porch and go straight on in.

Eric is sitting on the couch.

Jackknife is on the floor over by the front picture window. He's on his back, looking straight up at the ceiling. He has a gun in his right hand. There is a growing puddle of blood around his neck.

The blood is coming from an ugly gash in his throat.

I glance at Eric.

He is still holding the knife. He is staring at a blank TV screen and working his dry lips.

"Evil," he says. "So evil."

Chapter Thirty-nine

It's two AM. Eric and I are sitting in his kitchen at his table, drinking his beer. It's one of those light beers they advertise during football games. I think it tastes okay, but my Ice House is better.

Josh and the other kid had left about a half hour ago. They'd taken Jackknife's body with them. They told Eric they were going to dump him with his knife and gun. They said not to worry about it. Jackknife had had it coming for a long time, and that there were a lot of people laying for him, including Beto. Going to be some happy people when they find out he's gone, including Beto who seems to have changed his mind about Jackknife's story after he'd talked to me.

Neither of them would look at me nor come near me. They acted as though I didn't exist. The one with the broken nose had cleaned his face in the bathroom. The one named Josh wobbled a little from the sparks in his head.

Eric says to me, "Place in Tacoma I can get into a program and clean up. Becky says I can come see her if I'm straight."

I nod.

"Takes a while," he continues, "way I feel right now, I want to distance myself from this life, far as I can get."

"Jackknife maybe could have taken me straight up," I say. "I probably owe you one, so if you need any help."

"Thanks," he says. "I really don't know what got into me. Frustration, and feeling trapped, you know. He really was an evil person. But I don't think I meant to kill him. I just wanted to stop him. Just stop him. He was watching out the window and holding his gun and he was laughing like he was enjoying some sort of evil game being played in my driveway. I don't know." He shakes his head. "I saw where he'd left his knife on the coffee table. I picked it up and called his name, and when he turned I lashed out at him. It was really more of an accident, than anything, but I wanted with all my heart to stop him."

I sip my beer.

Eric sips his and swallows and says, "He was going to shoot you. He'd already gathered up his stash. Bout an ounce of product and a couple of stolen guns. He'd already put them in Josh's car. He was going to blow you away and leave me with the heat." He shakes his head again.

I notice his hands trembling as he takes another pull on his beer.

"Killing a person is easy," I rasp. "Living with it is another matter. Doesn't make any difference whether they had it coming or not. You'll remember this for the rest of your life, but it will get easier to live with after a while. Main thing is to get clean and stay that way. Becky loves you. I have a strong feeling that if you show up straight, she'll take you back."

"Really?"

"Yea. I really believe she will."

"I made a total mess of what we had."

I shrug, and we're quiet for a moment, and then I remember something about Becky that was always a puzzle to me, so I ask, "How come Becky never wanted to talk about getting a job? She avoided that subject. I never understood that part about her."

Eric smiles. "She's never had one, man. She ran away from home when she was seventeen. Started living with men, taking care of their needs. All she knows is how to cook, look pretty and have sex."

I stare at him as I think about that.

"But I love her, and I think she loves me. Hope I can win her back."

"I think you will," I say as I toss off my beer and rise from the chair.

We don't say goodbye.

Chapter Forty

I fall asleep in my easy chair around four. I'm holding
Pam's ring in my hand, and I'm thinking about taking it
to her. I dream about it.

I remember how Pam started going to church toward
the end of her life. I went with her a few times. I prayed hard
for her, and when I realized she was going to die anyway, I
told her our praying in church had done us no good.

She smiled and told me she hadn't been praying for a
longer life, just a better place to go at the end of it.

I think she is there.

We meet up in the court yard with the roses, in the
sunshine with a warm wind pushing the hem of her summer
dress around. She looks great. All the color is back in her
face and her hair is blond again. Her eyes are soft and blue
and full of light.

I try to hand her the ring, but she shakes her head at me.

I try to take her in my arms, but she disappears.

The phone wakes me at ten.

It's Becky.

"Eric called," she says. "Thank you for helping him. I knew you would."

"I didn't do much."

"It was enough. He told me you gave him some good advice too."

I say nothing.

"You're a man's man, Matt Conner."

I shake my head. "How's it going with your aunt and uncle?"

"Better than I thought it would. Not great, but you were right when you said it wouldn't hurt me."

"Good."

"See you around, old man."

"Maybe," I say, and we hang up.

The day slips away.

I'm not sure what all I do.

I know I tinker with the Mustang, and think about Pam. I know I shower and shave. I do a load of laundry, and I make a trip to Safeway for some groceries, and that's about it.

I'm sitting in my easy chair watching an ugly college football game when Faye calls.

"Matt, we need to talk."

"Yea, I guess we do," I say.

She hesitates. "Just got back from Ocean Shores. Jack's gone home to talk to his wife. Tell her about us. He doesn't think she'll fight a divorce. Their marriage hasn't been going so well anyway."

I nod.

"I don't want you to feel used," she blurts. "You scared me a little. I saw a part of you I'd not met."

"I know that," I say as I think about asking her what she'd expected me to do the night Jack wanted to see her, but I remember the evening gown, and I guess that pretty much sums it up.

"I don't know if it's going to work out with Jack," she says.

"How did it go at Ocean Shores?"

"It was..."

I wait.

"I told him I will not be his mistress," she says.

I scratch my chin.

She sighs, "I want a permanent relationship. What you and I had was enjoyable, but our arrangement made me realize something about myself. Am I making any sense?"

"Yes."

"I'm sorry."

"I am too, and I hope it works out for you with Jack."

"Thank you, Matt."

"Yup."

We hang up.

I fetch a beer from the fridge. An Ice House. I sit in my easy chair and I watch the game. Way I see it, Faye's conscience is bothering her.

It shouldn't.

I'm good with the way things turned out.

Before I know it, it's nearly dark and I'm on my second beer when someone knocks on my door.

I rise and walk over and open it.

Autumn is standing on my porch. She is wearing white shorts and a lime green blouse. She is pretty and she smells nice. She is holding a bottle of wine.

I smile.

She says, "Where were we before we were interrupted."